The DUSKHOUSE

And other Deceits

First Edition, Paperback – published 2013
Twisted Knickers Publications

ISBN: 978-0-9910027-1-9

Printed in the USA

Cover Art: *Abandoned Shacks* Coosa Valley Alabama NARA by Irving Rusinow 1941. Public Domain image courtesy of Wikimedia Commons.org
Cover Image Editing and Design By Twisted Knickers Imaging Services.

To Len

&

To All the Wonderful Editors who were kind enough to publish my twisted tales.

&

To the Flash Fiction Community for your enthusiastic support.

CHERYL ANNE GARDNER

The DUSK HOUSE

And other Deceits

A TWISTED KNICKERS PUBLICATION

THE DUSKHOUSE

I sat there, in the cold barren light of the full moon, looking at my scars. It all started with the party pills and ended in the dirty basement of a nearby haunted house.

I had arrived somewhere, early in the evening, somewhere loud and bright. Somewhere throbbing and sweaty and a little frightening. I met him there — wherever there was — pressed up against a smooth slick surface while we waited and admired all the pretty colored glass. He called me his French Kitty and smiled just right. He talked about curing diseases and the squalor of the ghetto. He said he was from Warsaw, said it with an accent. I giggled. I don't even know where Warsaw is. He gave me a little velvet box fastened with black ribbon and offered me something sweet — brittle white icicle sugar, he called it — dusting the cuff of his sleeve. There was a spider in the box ... and then I was in the box.

I awoke to a mouthful of dust and footsteps on the stairs, shuffling towards me in the gloom. I wished I could see better in the dark, but when the footsteps finally reached me, I wished I couldn't.

MARGARITAS AND RAZOR BLADES: AFTER FIVE PORNO FOR SKEPTICS

Tonight I am meeting a man who calls himself Mr. Oblivion. It's not really a date, and I am not exactly sure what I am going to say to him, if I need to say anything to him at all. I wasn't afraid in so many unsaid words, but I was reticent, as one should be when one is finally going to get to look into the black hard gaze of the man who plans to leverage your soul.

He was a collector: vomit, hair, toenail clippings, even menstrual blood. This time he said he wanted bone right down to the marrow. I wasn't sure I was ready to go that far, but he'd called it in, and so I didn't really have a choice.

I put some lipstick on my cigarette while he just watched me cross and uncross my leather-clad legs. We sat like that for hours before anything was said, before the terms of our arrangement were acknowledged, which he did so by showing his mettle. The hard edge caught in my eye as the grubby bar light glinted off it when he pulled it out of the little black satchel at his feet along with a pair of florescent orange nitrile gloves.

"For the cavity search," he said with a platinum grin. He didn't want to just spring it on me like that, but his internet connection had gone down last night before we'd had a chance to finish our little chat. The thread had just gone dead, and I thought that was how it was supposed to be. "No contact," he'd typed as his last words.

People are strange when it comes to what they think they own. I'd always thought what I possessed was mine, in a physical sense. I didn't believe that anymore. The first time we met, he'd reshuffled my thoughts on all this with a butane torch and a nail gun. He was going to save me from myself so that I didn't just end up a body inside a suitcase tossed in swamp one day.

"Did you bring it?" he asked, and I handed him the plastic baggie of leftover motel soap. He wanted to know that I was clean, wanted to see my pubic hair stuck to the crusted-over lather. He would use it to wash the blood off his gloves later.

The first couple of times, I felt a little disappointed that he wouldn't touch me without the gloves, but he said he never took anything for granted. He didn't want to taint me with his scent or his flesh. "I don't want to love you or rape you," he said. "I simply want to slit your lovely white throat."

THE SHADOW FACTORY

She never needed to reload.

It had only been a week, and you said the word "bed" with the wide innocent eyes of a child as in "Are we going to?" and she really didn't know what to say to you. She could see your expectant smile shining in the darkness, could feel your heartbeat thrumming the dead air of silence around her, but there were no words. Not for you.

She knew what you wanted, could feel it under your skin when you fucked her on the lino in the kitchen and against the dumpster in the parking lot and on the roof of your wife's car. Yes, she could feel it, and she wanted to cut it out, wanted to find you in the morning, a distant dream, a sigh that barely brushed up against the linen, but it was just too soon. She'd made the same mistakes before...

Mathew 7:16 wouldn't kiss her on the mouth even after she'd sucked the fuck out of him. "Selfish," she thought, every single time he came. His blood was slow and thick and tasted of tequila and mothballs.

Sometimes the dead speak to her. She would strip the sheets from the mattress and lie amongst them naked, listening to their complaints in the dark, the streetlights through the blinds marking the room off like the scene of a homicide. Sweat, and piss, and shit, and vomit. She could smell them all, taste them all, on the soft folds beneath her body.

Jake 5:22 would never look at her when he came. He

called her by his mother's first name when he fucked her, and then he'd call her a whore. "Too needy," she thought every single time he refused to look at her cunt. His blood was slick and gritty and tasted of grease.

Simon 3:18 would only ever fuck her in the ass. Said it looked like a nice tight schoolboy's ass. There was no blood in his veins.

You were different though, one week three days and you couldn't help but say the words, even if you didn't mean it. But you'd have to mean it, before you could join her here, in this private space between hope and pain.

You'd have to make her believe it, before she could ever accept your stain.

BIKE TRAILS AND ASH CLOUDS

You just have to let the hunger take what it needs and love what it loves.

I love you.
Simply.

I don't even know what love means or how to do it. You robbed me of that.

I hear the sound of running water, or it might be the sound of blood running down the length of me.

How pretentious, you, offering me a light ... a drink ... and then a ride home.

Is it because I can't dance?

How did you know I couldn't dance? I've been sitting here all night. Yes. I'm an introvert, it's obvious to me, but when you say it, it sounds so thin.

Pointless.

We're both awkward, but even so, your advances are suspect. Lewd. Just the way I like them, but I don't tell you that. You said, "Hey. Remember that fat girl from high school? The one they called miss kitty because she liked to finger herself in the shower after gym class?" and I said, "That was me."

You'd taken her panties. Left her crying on the football field when you promised to kiss her and then didn't. It was just a random moment in time. You told everyone you'd fucked her though, and that she liked it.

Everyone laughed.

At her.

Not you.

I used an alias on my nametag tonight. You couldn't have known it was me. I'm thin, beautiful now, and you're ... not. I saw you slip that powder into my drink. A few minutes ago, when I went to freshen up. Some things never change, but I'm immune to your charms now. You couldn't know that, either. I wasn't then, so in the end, assumption would be your undoing. Not mine.

"Oh, how silly of me; now I'm being pretentious."

That's what I'll say to you. Just before I shut the trunk so I won't have to hear you begging. It's the silence I'm after. I'll seek comfort tonight, in the moon … and in the dream I once had of you screaming. I'll smile. I'll revel in the small comforts, offered, until now never taken. Just like I did all those years ago on that cold lonely football field where you and your scumbag friends scarred me for life.

You were the first, so how could I not still love you?

Look—

I'm a snow angel now. Thanks for lending me your skin to make my wings. I hope the thought of *me* doesn't haunt *you* anymore.

HEY SHITBAG, WHAT'S *MY* DESTINY?

You hit a nerve, made my hands shake when you grazed those painted nails across my arm. The way you shook your ass at me and that peek-a-boo on the sly when you bent over and let me get a good look at your cunt from behind.

> You made me make a sacrifice,
> For you,
> Not me.

I hated the thought of your smile and your fake pouty lips, but I loved the commune of your flesh, shared and tattered. You gave it a bad rap. Your life, you said. It was just porno and tap water, malted milk balls and restless cocks. You called yourself Destiny, and I wondered why someone like you would work in a chicken house like this. Maybe you was mad at your daddy. Hope I didn't look like him, so I sat at the back of the bar, in the dark, contemplating your full lips and how they would look severed from your face and mounted on my throbbing cock. You said you could see the future in that little deck of cards you carried around in your purse, said it with a "Hey Mister," when you asked me if I wanted to know mine. "Ten bucks," you said, and I replied, "Divine."

You thought I was talking about you, but I wasn't. I asked what you did for a living while I flipped the tassel on your boob, and you said you liked to fuck. "With a crystal ball?" I asked, and you laughed at me. You didn't want to know what I did, what my passion was. You said it was all in the cards, and that death with his rusted out scythe and his emerald green eyes was just a beginning. I nodded and fingered the razor in my pocket, 'cause I supposed it was true. Well, you believed it, along with the moon and the stars and the voodoo priestess who told you "you" had a gift. You didn't want to know about all the naughty things little girls like you shouldn't know about. You didn't want to know about my fascination with skin.

I am a sculptor.
What's inside you is weak,
And I can fix it –
With plaster.

I want to fuck you with a chisel. Scrape the ligaments from your bones. What I do is a labor of love. I bring things back to life, but you didn't even really want to know me beyond the free drinks and the bits of coin I dropped in your tip jar. You thought you were a hipster, a girl gone wild, but you're really just a fucking parsley-smoking bigot, getting back at her rich drunk daddy. Your bust will look nice mounted next to the saw palmetto by the shed. I'll use pencil erasers to keep your nipples hard, yet supple. That's what I was thinking while you giggled and practiced your "witchcraft," as you liked to call it. You went on and on about sinkholes and bedbugs and why it's so important to wash the fucking sheets. What if I default on my lottery payments? Will I get sued for all those vile accusations I made about the frigid bitch of a mayor? Or was I letting failure bloom when I spread my seed to the hookers on the next street corner? "Fuck no," I replied. "This is a small town, honey, and there ain't no jobs in this dust-storm famine funeral parlor. I got clients. Not a lot of hunting to do around here, you see, so I might be easy money, but this strip ain't the only game in town." You smiled again, said I was hokey and quaint. Wanted to know whether I wanted to smoke a joint and get a lap dance or not. Now, I don't know nothing bout your big city ways with your tattoos and pierced clits and all that greasy black eye makeup. I just skin them and stuff them; well, you don't really stuff them, not like a scarecrow with sawdust and hay.

I do like your sky blue innocent eyes, though.

I think I'll keep them for myself.

A SACK OF RAGS AND ROCKS

I can still smell the perfume in their hair — the scent of lavender just after a summer rain — as it drifted to me across the ice. The lake had frozen that January, under the midnight moon, and neither a pound of gold nor the beating heart of a love struck man could raise the dead, drifting on the current just below the surface. I knelt down and gazed at the reflection of my love in their cold dead eyes. I wanted to chisel away at their beauty now more than ever, their innocence a glittering prize, but the ice was too thick now. I'd spoken of my desires often, in secret, whispered to no one but the only one I trust. "You might have had the splendor, but never the virtue," the ugly old shrew advised me through rotted teeth and needful breath as she looked at the spread of cards laid out before her, "And neither would have made you happy in the end."

She only wanted the best for me, so I don't know why I expected her to understand my infatuations. She wasn't a faith healer ... She was just my mother — a witch and a whore — and she never told me the water would be so cold.

ME, YOU, AND THEY

I drink the sound of you — begging
In the darkness.
Begging for what I've given,
And for what you've taken — from me.
And I pray now for the silence
To overtake
Your blackened heart.

You didn't know that's what I was writing on that piece of parchment stained with your blood. Things have been a blur lately, all emotions, anger, and don't touch me because I'll scream. It wasn't the first piece of parchment I'd burned and buried under the light of the full moon, but it would be the last. The last words I would never speak to you.

"You clumsy fucking worthless piece of shit!" was not the only peevish and pedantic phrase you used to scream into my face after a long night of booze and pills and dangling your cock at every skanky twat working the freeway. Your dinner was cold. You didn't like the way I vacuumed the carpet or cooked your special meat. I might have forgotten to record your favorite program, or maybe I'd simply bought the wrong kind of beer. You liked to call it an intervention, when you humbled me with your fist. Said it would make me a better lady, wife, and someday — mother. Said the discipline would save my soul from the voodoo spirits that had borne me out of some trailer trash womb, but it wasn't an intervention, and it wouldn't save me. It was simply your way of justifying the use of all the angry words you had become addicted to.

I didn't have to listen, though.

I had this place I liked to hide whenever you got in one of your moods and decided to kick start a marital uprising. I liked to go there when it was dark and snow covered. I prayed there, sobbed there, and bled there. In the dirt on the floor, I would scratch things down in inches of minutia and then straightaway cross them out. I would leave pieces of myself in the corners — dissected thoughts and bits of hair and fingernails mixed with mud and saliva. I've piled up the worry stones over the years, on the stoop and up in the eves. I'd even written and re-written your obituary and passed the judgments I wasn't entitled to pass, but nothing ever happened.

Nothing good, anyway.

Just dark, and cold, and quiet.

Maybe it was like they said, when the shadows came to me hollow-eyed in the misty dawn. Maybe I wasn't soulful enough, hungry enough, willful enough ... to leave the memories well enough alone, but I wouldn't stop trying.

Praying of them.

Begging mercy of them.

I took your hair and fingernails while you slept. Scraped your semen from my bloody cunt when you finally said you'd had enough of me. I'd even collected your fallen eyelashes when I pretended I loved you and kissed you softly, and your spit when, in anger, it hit my face. I stood in the circle, called the watchtowers, and drew down the moon a thousand times since we took our vows. Since then I vowed to put you in your grave. I thought I might try arsenic and old lace. It grew wild and beautiful in the abandoned field behind our house. That's when they first came to me, when I was barefoot, gathering weeds in the wood. They said they wanted the meat, but I didn't know what they meant by that. *Just the meat — no hair, no bone, no gristle. Only meat.* So I made offerings: rats, chickens, even your dog. Gutted it with my bare hands in the mid-day sun, but I got nothing in return, except a beating — from you.

Until now.

I went to the shed, you see. Even though you told me not to, ever. I found your "things," wondered how many you'd tortured before me. I couldn't remember you ever being this quiet when I put the claw hammer in your skull. Couldn't remember you being this heavy when you lay on top of me, or that your skin was this tough. I was clumsy, like you always said, hacking away at you until the sun was set and the crickets had started chirping in the field. I lit a candle with my bloodied hands and just stared at your meat in the flickering light. You looked different to me then. I could finally see a softness in your glistening sinews.

They came for you that night, finally. After all the years and all my tears, they came, clicking and clawing their way out of the shadows to gnaw upon your rotted meat. They were hungry and waiting ... for me.

I would never starve them like you did.

CHOKE

It started as an itch, burnin, festerin until the hate broke the skin and slithered out. It was like this every time, and I didn't like doin it.

My momma always said, "If you don't like somethin, change it." She never said nothin about can't. Can't was a bad attitude, won't was even worse. I didn't like neither of them words. She made me eat green soup with chunks of fat in it, or at least I think it was fat. "Hocks," she called it, showed me where it were on a body, poked it with an iron rod and said you gotta smoke em up so's they don't taste nasty and tough.

Those were tough times. I was a kid then, spent my days dustin the tombstones in the abandoned churchyard behind my house. Sometimes I'd find bones that had risen to the surface after a hard rain. The crows would pick them up 'cause they're shiny and then drop them on the porch. I liked to drill holes in them and hang them from the apple tree gone dead in the yard. Lots of things gone dead here.

There was this dream I had once, the moon hangin low overhead as the night collected around my feet, swirlin and swallowin up my shadow. I was runnin across a starlit skyline, jumpin from rotted rooftop to rotted rooftop in this podunk town. I'd been around the world, you see, had the stamps to prove it, stuck to my flesh, all cancelled and faded. The adhesive would give me a painful itch sometimes, but it was worth it. Below me, inside the walls of sleep where the soot and seepage couldn't touch them, the townsfolk went undisturbed. I often wished I were like them, warm and comfortable, but I'm not. Tonight, momma sent me out to get the hocks. She showed me how to put em down, how to lock my fingers and twist – hard. I get hurt sometimes. They kick and squeal, and I hate them 'cause there ain't never enough meat on them anyway. Other parts is better, but momma says they's dirty. Makes me bury them in the boneyard, where my daddy is, but sometimes I don't. I won't.

But I don't say anythin. I just sit and eat my green soup, hatin on her, wishin I was the wind. I knew I'd never be. Momma said she needed a man around to smoke the meat, but if I could, just for a minute – that minute when they'd finally stop breathing – I'd be swingin from the weathervanes, just like I did in that dream.

CINEMA NOIR

Your shadow bumped into mine in that cold dark alley. When you held that knife to my throat and said you wanted me in slow malingering spit-drenched words. I kissed you then, soft on the lips. No tongue. Just a breath of what was to come. You wanted to finger my slit, but I wouldn't let you, said it wasn't for you – not yet. Your cock was out, shimmering wet in the streetlight ... and the rain. When I looked up, you smiled at me, slit my throat just a little, and smeared the blood on yourself until you came. You cried out, "Jesus! I fucking love you," but I was already gone, slipped away into the shadows, my memory of you a forgotten stain, left to the rats ... and the roaches. I'll find you again someday, and this time, this time I'll have rope enough to bind you.

DEPUTY LARRY

It's a lovely trick, isn't it? Hauling up the bodies.

Larry always wanted to "poke them with a stick" after they'd washed up on the banks of the river, blue and bloated, looking like over-boiled meat, all slagging skin and maggots.

That sort of thing pushes the hard line, makes you forget the bit of blandness in your day. Most days you can get past it, even the smell. If you try hard enough, that is. There ain't nothin' five kegs of burgundy wine can't do for a jittery soul, but Larry was different. Larry could wait it out. He always had five great tips for jet lag, and yet, he had never flown a day in his life. He was on the no-ride list because of an incident in Topeka, and so his detention in this podunk town had been extended to life with no possibility of parole. But he didn't mind — the absence from himself. He was born on notice, a bit unhinged in the horseshoe hut, if you get my drift, but when he hit it, he hit back and hard. He just didn't like things too bright, would always crinkle up his nose when the sun hit his face, and he'd spend hours with a jar of coal tar, polishing his badge, which he said was the shiniest of shinies. We never let him carry a gun after Topeka, but then again, he never asked to. He'd just stand over the bodies, stick in his hand.

"This is what happens when love is all you got left," he would say, and Larry was always right. He always knew who they were ... where they'd been...

And who had loved them last.

THE CLIPPER, THE CLOWN, AND A BAG OF DARK DIRTY THINGS.

He offered her a zombie cocktail, the suave motherfucker with his metro accent and his glassy-eyed laissez affair. I sat there and watched like it was a personal affront, burning the cello wrapper on my cigarette pack until it curled up into a blackened waxy ball I could flip at the waitress who'd been ignoring me for almost an hour. There will come a time when the illusion becomes real and you believe everything is grey cheese and fickle brain-eating amoebas, warning us about the rat-pig rodent winter coming to a mass murder near you. I could kiss off all the criticism and consumer media, 'cause this new addiction I got falls just short of ear splitting ecstasy.

She was decked out in X-rated warning labels and firecrackers. She was as deadly as the switchblade strapped to her thigh. It made me jealous the way she toyed with the proper Johns as if she were something, something other than what she was once, back in the dust bowl...

It was a season of extremes, seeing her here, a hitchhiker resurrection in hotel gift shop linens.

NEW AND IMPROVED TEN-IN-ONE KOOTCH claimed the gargantuan sign over my head as the barker staked his claim with a red, orange, and white painted banner. We'd had the only show like it, but that was years ago, years best forgotten. I thought I'd seen the last of it, the last of her, but the sexy billboard off the interstate said otherwise. You'd think I would have learned by now that you never see the last of anything. Damn fancy-pants billboard advertisers! How do they know who you are? What you're looking for? I hadn't been on the circuit in years. Neither had she. She'd got tired of it all, the cheers and the jeers, the foul subtext, and all the creepy flophouse men. She'd got tired of being applauded with ignorance and vomit, so she made a bid and hit the dirt road in a turnip truck on its way to LA.

She'd had work done: liposuction, a little electrolysis, organic foods and herbal supplements. Throw in one silicone implant, a careful tuck, and a whole lot of clean living, and there she was, rubbin' up against the beautiful people. Her days of walking with the dead were over, history, just a rotten childhood memory best left to the imagination of horror fiction writers and fetish freaks.

She had real style now, all capped teeth, kinky boots, and a shaved ass. She'd hit the majors. I settled farther into the shadows at the back of the room. Smoked my cigarette. I was used to it. The silence. The fear on their faces. No one ever looked directly at me, let alone looked me in the eye, no one except her. I missed her, and I hated the way the men looked at her. She'd finally figured out how much she was worth and had bid the gaffs a fond adieu for good.

She wasn't just a sideshow anymore, she was an "act." Things weren't the same without her. I flipped open my tired old leather satchel. They were all rusty and dull. Everything was, until now. I might grow tired of watching her, someday, but for now, I'll keep at it until she screams or begs me to stop.

THE LEGACY AND A HOT PINK EDDY

I was travelling on a train through Sweden, but the mountains flashing past me through the window reminded me of the Carpathian mountains, draculated and moody, the mist collecting at the tops of the trees where the shadows hung unseen in the dawn. I'd had some brandy and some meat pie. Liver and prunes heated with a bit of pâté brisee. I felt I should be writing in my journal but my fingers felt like sticks of meat. Mutton. Rotted and gangrened mutton. I'd lost my passport somewhere in Munich, and had to hitch a ride with Bjorn, the delirious dentist who liked scraping his toenails with a dental pick and drilling holes in his own teeth for fun. We were quite the pair. He the society derelict inhaling a bit of rustic pleasure, and me, a bashful yet aggressive forbidden thing who'd forgotten herself somewhere during the last full moon. I was one of The Rapture's leftovers, strutting my slayer shit like it was a courtesy not a curse.

I was a Van Helsing, so I said was my destiny, though I wasn't sure whether knowing that was an inspiration, a victory, or just a stalemate between what I needed and what I desired. I'd been hunting for a while, and I took the dating rules seriously. I wasn't just a heckler in a crowd of pork rinds, pop-corn blondes, and sperm donors. I was in it for real, but I needed bone marrow with deep roots, no Bella Lugosi knockoffs for me. That's why I was running, chasing shadows around the world and back again with Dr. Dementia over there.

The last one was a disaster...

We'd met at one those meat packing warehouse raves. He was glowing in the strobe lights. Pale, handsome, his nails — painted black — shimmered like flickering stars. He pressed me up against the wall in the alley. He felt heavy and cold, colder than the wall, and he was eerily brazen, so I told him to shove it.

"I wanna suck it and fuck it," he said when I kissed the frigid skin of his neck.

"Do what you will," I told him. "I can't stand you, and I don't fucking care."

He said he liked the wild ones and that I had "spirit." Said I looked like I was worth a taste. Then he said he was a thousand years old as if it made any difference to me. It didn't. I pulled out the three-foot stainless steel and African Mahogany stake I had hidden in my trench coat, and he just said, "Kinky, but what am I supposed to do with that?"

"I don't know," I said. "Fuck it, suck it. Do what I tell you to do with it. You are my darkness. I love you, and I can't deny you, but I won't ever fucking say so."

He fondled my tits. Pinched my nipples through my bra. Then forced his hand down my panties and grabbed my cunt. He said he wanted to suck it and fuck it again, whispered it, with hot spit on his lips, and I told him, "Do what everyone else expects you to do. I feel indifferent, and you care too damn much about your image to think for your fucking self."

He backed up, threw his hands in the air, and then called me a tease, a bitch, and a whore, to which I replied quickly and without words. Thwump! A swift kick to his chest. A gurgling exhale, and the sound of a hammer against steel, echoing off the wet brick walls left the moon with little recompense.

The boy looked surprised, his black eyeliner running down his face. He just kept saying, "Fuck fucking fuck," while grabbing and tearing at his oozing chest.

"Nosferatu," I screamed. "Fucking piece of maggot riddled shit." That's what he was, with a bad suit and a gold card, no less. I'm never wrong about these things. I bent over and smiled at him. "It's wet, and dark, and cold, and you know it. Just like all the fucking promises you whispered to me when we met."

It's hollow, he replied. I'm hollow.

"And you are a miserable excuse of a monster."

There isn't enough of me

To fill the empty space

I thought I had left

For you.

After that, every time I saw a full moon, I would think of that night long ago. I would think of Milan in the spring and all the blood splatter everywhere.

Until now.

Now the dentist drills their teeth out for me so I can wear them around my neck. He's not bad company, really, and he makes damn sure I never fall in love again.

THE STRANGE SICKNESS OF STAN WORCHKOWSKY

He set the timer on the microwave to 6.66 and pressed the start button.

Stan Worchkowsky worked the night shift, and it was just as well. It was the only time he could turn it off, the only time he could mute the ads and block the banners that bombarded his head with static almost twenty-four hours a day. He couldn't stop watching. Not with his eyes, but with his mind, rapt, in old bloody newsprint and fish guts and hate. He felt he lived an outer life of hidden inner thoughts and messages, of voices cluttered with codes and signs and predictions for the future. The night shift offered him a moment of peace and quiet. No one wanted to work in the darkness where strange and beautiful creatures lie naked and alone, knowing only death and the horrors that lie beyond it.

Stan Worchkowsky worked in reclamations. No security cameras. No contracts. No negotiations. Just a floor drain and a steel slab.

Number 38765 was a Hep C. He liked to look at them in particular, liked to touch their cold flesh and stare into their jaundiced eyes. Daisies. Eyes like daisies. He liked to pop them out and put them in the microwave. Liked to snip bits off here and there, the parts he favored. The black market gems. The flawed ones might get you a pint or two, a grotesque might make a mortgage payment, and the amber liquid, if it was fresh, had a street value worth its weight in gold. The stock market never had returns like that.

He could remember the stock market.

Nobody even played the stocks anymore, except the fucking junkie assholes who were always trying to break in and suck the meat dry. That's why he worked the night shift. He didn't have to feed like they did. He had held out when everyone else had started gnawing on each other, so he could be picky with the scraps.

Grade A.

He refused to reclaim anything less. Oh people would pay for less, would kill for less if they had to — if they had the thirst and the hunger. Sometimes he envied them ... at least they didn't have the static.

A MURDER ON THE BANKS OF THE SEINE

It was not yet properly dawn, just a meager, swollen yellowish light, and the earth was wet and cold, full of tangled roots, rocks, and worms. The sewer rats had torn your toenails off ages ago as you clawed and scrapped your way through the mud. You had drunk your fill at the banquet hall, had leered at the servants while feasting on baskets of bloody shrimp. Now your body aches, and you feel the hours poisoning your mind. Someone had covered your naked flesh with a quilt sewn of misty roses, misery, and clouds, but you can't remember who had done it or when. Was it before the chanting, or after?

You just can't remember, the candles fractured heat had long been spent, and there you lie, a languid image struggling against the dawn.

I had finished with you.

Finished with us.

I was tired of swallowing water every time I breathed you in.

The gravel had left its hateful memory on my face and on my chest, but I continued heaving dirt into the hole with my bare hands as lightning split the sky off in the unthinkable distance.

It was nothing like yesterday.

I'd stayed too long, trying to make amends, your corpse stinking and rotting in the heat of the sun surrounded by a field of pastel trifles, your melancholia and your lapses of time and reason set to the baleful librettos of Wagner still fresh in your mind, or rather, what was left of it after the meat cleaver.

You'd lied to me. Tricked me into thinking I was a lady, but my cunt is just as rotted as my liver and my kidneys and my heart. Why do women have to fight to find their place? That was often how the conversation started, just as often as I'd find myself standing naked in front of the mirror, poking and prodding the mental and physical gelatin with all manner of tricky questions and even more complicated and elaborate answers. Supermodel, souvenir, or sex crime? What was I really ... to you? The absence was never visible, you see, no matter which way I turned or which dark, musky crevice I exposed to the light.

You liked to pretend you didn't notice me, noticing you, noticing how worn out I'd become. You smiled like you liked it when I called myself your wife, your lover, and your friend, but I was nothing more than a used up trollop with a bit of coin, gorging myself on sulky sweet-buttered smiles and secrets. Oh, but I had a secret for you. I'd made the pâté myself from the cyanide-poisoned rats I'd been collecting in the basement of your house. The house I wasn't supposed to know you have, on the side, with her.

I took those cooking lessons you suggested: a little garlic, a pound of bacon, some sweet heavy cream, and just a pinch of pepper and sea salt. I'd wrapped it up real fancy, told you it cost a small fortune. You'd brought candles and cheap wine. Kept licking the hairy meat off your lips while telling me it was the best you had ever tasted. You'd often said the same about me when you flayed my flesh three times a week in the dark. Oh yes, lover, you liked the look and feel of contentment – suck my cock, you said, like it was an aperitif – but you didn't look that way now. The black winged beggars had picked you starving and miserable. I know I shouldn't have left you there. I thought no one had seen, but they had, and they came for you at dawn and at dusk, a swirling obsidian mass of hunger, hypnotized by your bulging bloodshot eyes.

ELIGIBLE BACHELOR

A lady in white, who used to be my lady, sits silently upon a marble bench in the churchyard of my youth, a silver ladle lying in the wet grass at her feet, stale frosting and cake crumbs dusting her lips and her breasts.

It was an anxious, tormented love, she felt for me, like a cold rain chastening her heart. She had defined it so often, justified it more often than that.

She had ventured into the churchyard that cold and clammy November morn, had walked a mile of grey shadows and stone. It was a misstep, once made, and she couldn't help but look up at me as she tumbled down, down, and down the moonlit shaft into the crypt below, white orchids clenched tightly in her hands.

In this quiet place, she could forget, could forget the loneliness and time. Could forget me, and I her. Or so she thought. You see, the churchyard was filled with the wounded, and she belonged there, certainly, but there was no place for her, not while she still felt alive.

And so I would wait, six months, a year, until the screaming stopped, then I would come back to her, when she had lost all hope, when the chill had set permanently into her bones. She would want me then, and I would have forgiven her her refusals.

You think me odd, but a woman needs time to come to her senses. In the gloaming, she was not without her loveliness. The grey slag of her skin shimmering in the torch light, she seemed less bitter now, less brittle than a day without rain ago.

"I brought champagne, my dear."

Her lips said yes.

Her whole body said yes. The lace in her bodice disintegrated, the blue veins in her breasts flushed with moonlight as she stared into the distance she knew only as me.

She begged me take her, begged like she'd never had before as the shadows, spun from cobwebs and tears, collected in the damp corners and empty spaces around us.

They would bear witness, finally, to our love and to our only moment of wedded bliss.

I hated to leave her. Hated to deceive her, but I desired another. So fickle are the passions of a man, and eventually, she, too, would find herself here — waiting. They all do. Waiting for me to touch them, to love them just a little.

RED RIDING

You smiled at me because I couldn't fold a fitted sheet, and I laughed at you because your "whites" were grey. You read steampunk, and I read smut. We'd swap sentences under the flickering florescent lights. The change machine was broken, so you went out in the rain to get more quarters at the Gas-N-Sip. You'd always bring back a slushy for me. My lips would turn blue, and you'd steal my panties, put them on your head, and parade around the launderette. I lost you to the waxing moon, and now, sitting alone in the dark, I realize this ... this the dishonest parting of my soul.

You accost me now with chaos; eject your black death into me. You stink of the sewer, of the shadows, and of the rats. You're a thrill seeker. A phantom. You say I am ugly when I cry. Then you make me cry. You were charming once ... at the launderette.

You say our love, it's been more complicated than expected, just short of an anagram, so I say, "Light the candles and make a list of what you need."

You ask if it can be personal – of wood with a hint of silver, and I say, yes.

I've called out to you from the cold, from snowdrifts and rotted trees, but you never answer me now. You just claw at my door and gut the neighbors' cat.

We'll meet again in the dark. In the confusion of us.

I'll bury you there. No one will know where.

It's what expected.

I'd warned you before, but you'll never see, the carnage that is you and the vengeance that is me.

BLEEDER

They slid the tray under the door with nothing upon it but lizards and gizzards – raw. They never came in. They were afraid to look at you. It was a comfortable distance to be separated – from them – from the hazy remembrance of what you once were.

Pressed against the dark and the cold, you often pretended you were sitting in a theatre, miles away from yourself. The plot of this danse macabre served no purpose other than to ridicule the random cruelty and suffering you had once called a life.

There's nothing left for you now. Nothing left but decades of emptiness.

You can hear the wind, the morning chill still clinging to its breath as it beckons you to the pyre, on this, an uneasy dawn. You ate the salamanders, fiery red, and you can feel them now crawling through your veins as you watch the listless shadows on the avenue swell to an orchestral mass. The moon is still full and bright and hateful in the sky as you look out towards your destiny through iron bars and sweating stone.

They are all there – the faces of the damned – staring back at you through the dimly lit eyes of the thousand lives you had long left behind. You wonder how many will weep for you in the hours you've left them. Not many, you imagine. You know them all too well. Their names are writ in blood on your heart and on your soul. They think they'll be rid of you when you're nothing but dust and ash. They think death can stop you, but it won't. You'll come for them eventually, all of them, before the breaking dawn. Their little trinkets won't save them. They know the truth, as close to the truth as they could ever get, clutching their superstitions tightly to their chests.

You remember the last. The sheets, wrinkled, when she left her mark upon them, when she gasped into the cotton fibers for last time before her eyes went dead from the shame. The loss was always painful for you. You wanted her, for a time, and she wanted you, or rather, she wanted an idea she had of you. She said she wanted it. Said she wasn't afraid. Said you were her dark angel and that she wanted to be devoured by the night. She was a child, her frailty concealed behind pouty red lips and fingernails painted black, but you weren't bitter, even if her eagerness was disappointing. You told her it would end soon, that the shine would fade. Then you watched as the rain fell upon the moonlit blue-black of her skin, watched her feeble pride betray her, again, and then harder, and then again. She begged you to spare her body, but you wouldn't. She was too needy. She'd never survive eternity.

None of them could.

Now the city of Athens burns in your dreams, a waking dream made heavy by the rusted iron clasped to your bruised ankles and wrists.

You only ever bled them a little. What crime was there in that?

RAW SEWAGE

One of the biggest mistakes he'd ever made was licking that light post, the one just outside the X-rated theatre on Delaney Street.

He'd attended church that night at the chapel down the road, said, "The sermon set my hair afire," and he meant it, literally. I heard rumor that it did just that, struck by lightning, right there in the breach between a Hail Mary and an Our Father. His appeal had been turned away, his faith decapitated and found later in a ditch off Highway 1.

He claimed in a hysterical confession that a school nurse had touched him—there—during her "inspections," which involved Polaroids and cherry flavored lollies and lube.

"Women shouldn't act like men," he said, but she did — look like a man — even with everything tucked out of sight. He said he could smell gasoline and sewage in her hair, when it wasn't pinched tight to her head, when she'd hovered low over him and he could feel it against the naked skin of his back. She'd said all girls had spicy secrets and that all boys loved that sort of thing. That's why he'd licked the light post. That was the first night he saw her again. She was older, yes, a little worn, but it was her, definitely her, in her nurse's outfit, pushing the edges, pawning her favors in the throbbing red light.

She'd rubbed her bare ass up against that light post, ever so briefly, and this time, he'd wanted something to keep.

RED LIGHTS AND JADE PAINT

"Drop your gear, bend over, and show me what you got."

That's what he said to her, and then he smiled a crack house rot smile of contentment so powerful he got hard in his pants. He'd known her for a long time. Could never be with her – in public – like this – so intimately and so perfectly – but this was fine, for the both of them. He watched the sequined thong slide down her leg to her silky-smooth delicate ankle as he reached into his jacket pocket for his little spray bottle of Windex. He squirted it on the Plexiglas and buffed his view of her to a brilliant shine. She looked so good when the glass was sparkling. So hot, bent over, the length of her hair spilling onto the shabby lacquered floor. She had a dragon tattoo on her ass, its tongue curved around her buttocks, gently licking at that place no man was allowed to go.

He wanted that dragon, wanted to feel its breath in flame and in ash, but he never would ... never could.

She turned around and sat down in her souped-up dentist's chair. He loved that chair so much, her tan skin slick against the white leather and chrome. "There's no rush, baby," she said as she put one leg up over each arm of the chair so he could see everything. He liked to look at her, liked to watch her touch herself with those jet-black painted fingernails. Oh, she knew what he wanted. They were in synch since the moment they'd met. She smiled at him again – no words – and then produced a tube of lipstick out of thin air it seemed. She tarted her lips up all fire-engine red and shiny against her wide white teeth. And then she licked them, like he'd often imagined she might lick a lollipop or a lamppost or a tire iron. She moaned a little, winked at him — because she knew that's exactly what he was thinking — and then she reached down to candy-apple gloss those other lips. The ones mamma said were special. The ones he didn't deserve — ever — not even on Christmas.

'detta never thought that way about him, though. They'd always had "this thing" between them, the way they could just be with each other in silence. He wanted to taste her, of course, smell her, feel her tight skin against his. He wanted her in a way that made him feel small and ashamed. She was all things. She was everything. She was Odetta Rouge, and he loved being in love with a whore.

"Fuck, fucking motherfucker," he shouted when he realized the razor in his coat pocket was sharper than he thought, and he cut his finger just before the blackout screen came down. Before the room went pitch and cold. He ached for her still, but he'd be with her again soon. "Not soon enough, but soon," he thought as he smeared his blood all over the glass where the image of her had once been. A perfect image, driven from his mind when the buzzer sounded and the little light above the door changed from red to green. He waited — with patience and in silence — one latex-gloved hand on the doorknob — for the latch to click clickety clack open to the dimly lit, red-velvet covered hall of his youth. He'd lost it here somewhere, his youth, tangled up in all the jasmine scented pubic hair and lust. He slipped the razor back in its sheath and made his way to the counter.

"Next Tuesday?" the leather-clad clerk behind the counter asked him just before he paid what was due and scheduled his next call in her queue. It was Christmas, and Tuesday was a long way away, he thought. The stainless steel in his pocket was too cold, and next Tuesday was too long for him to wait, perhaps. He'd been good this year. Too good not to admit it, and too good not to take what he'd earned.

THE DISQUIET OF DORIAN AND THE GREY

I looked down at the tattered and blood-soaked cuffs of my shirt, realizing that fortune and happiness aren't off the rack ready-to-wear. You need designer style and a want to do desperate things.

She was a wreck – all snarled hair and thin skin rubbing against bone – sipping gin from a teacup. It had been over two hours, and my canvas was scrawled with rage not paint.

"The rain washed my makeup off," she'd said when she arrived, shaking her umbrella as she walked in from the cold. Her feet were bare, and she giggled as the sleet slicked from her toenails to the creaking floorboards.

I'd been waiting. For what, I do not know. Maybe her, when I think about it now. She was an unexpected talent, and the bugs in my stomach squirmed against the whiskey and bacon I had eaten earlier for breakfast. The hunger shone in her, too. Her teeth looked like miniature marble pillars when she smiled, and she had a distance in her eyes – livid – like sex dipped in gunmetal and chocolate. She was a collision with cutlery, and I just had to paint her. Had to. Her filthy flesh was a feast awash in the fell light of the moon, and I felt a velvet hollowing in the center of all things, felt the paint as it congealed around the flattering silhouette that was she, who graced the dark corners of my mind.

She was a secret ... and when she giggled again and lifted her scars into the moonlight for me, I knew I would have to keep her that way – forever, and ever, forever.

MADAME MALICIOUS AND THE MOST UNLIKELY OF PEERS

Madame wouldn't release him until the autumn. Something about the chill damp air when the moon was full and high in the sky, cleaved by jagged cloud and mist. I suspected the scenario had something to do with her fetish for all things grey and meaty. It was a private fetish, handcrafted from rusted iron, dripping stone walls, and mirrors. I remember she said once that everyone was weighed down by lust coupled with time and gravity. She understood the equation. "The moon could relieve the pressure," she'd said, and I believed her. She was all risk, all impulse. A ruby-eyed obsession. I had fallen for her — hard. She was a different kind of problem for me. She was bleach and rat poison — a real palate cleanser. Before I met her, my life was all cheap wine and sleeping pill hangovers. A byline. That was before she became my mistress. Before I enjoyed the musty aroma of her breath and the way she hushed me when I cried out in the darkness.

She said I wasn't polluted like the others.

The first time I saw her was about a year ago. She'd crept out of the shadows into a luminescent altered state of moonlight and streetlight. She'd bent over — all the way over — and adjusted her stockings. Those legs she had ... those legs were purple plush and dripping red skies. In her sport leathers, she cut a handsome figure in the gloaming. She'd met him there, the first of many, on that lonely corner. He waived his cigar around for a while, blew smoke in her face, and then gestured towards the alley like she was a cheap trick. She wasn't. It all happened so fast, but I caught the look on her face with my camera. Caught the moon in her eyes. She'd seen me. She smiled and touched her throat, and then SNAP! The flash went off, startling him, so he grabbed her elbow and quickly ushered her into the dark. I'd fucked up with the flash, for sure. Gave myself away. I thought I would never see her again, so I blew up the photo of her lips — tacked it to the wall in the closet where I liked to touch myself and cut myself with little bits of tin and broken glass. Somehow, she knew. I photographed her every night after that ... until the grey changed.

She'd said she didn't like to color outside of the chalk lines, you see, not with crayon, or oil, or blood. She had a signature style, a motive all her own, but of late, a little bit of wanderlust had crept in. That's what she called it. "It's something that happens to you, something that overtakes you," she said. "The Hunger." It's what connects us all, and for that reason, she normally liked to eat locally and alone. The remains, those wretched bits of cartilage and bone, she tossed aside for the scavengers like me. She'd evolved, she said. Liked restoring order, and was ever careful, never fearful. That was before, though. Before the other came — from the dark into the light. Before the grey changed to panic and hysteria and chunks of skewered flesh left to rot in the sun. Before the pat-downs and the apologies — and before the inquisition alluded to anyone other than her — it was all scarlet burning and baptisms in the moonlit bay, but now, since the headlines had called them "killings" in the plural — the other's not hers — the tourists have deserted the streets, leaving the evening's hidden wonders to those who seek to indulge themselves with electric pitchforks and fluorescent lights.

She left me, cold dawn and wet pavement, with nothing more than a scratch to remember her by. I never told anyone her name. They call that journalistic integrity, but in reality, for all the time she'd spent clawing and gnawing at my flesh, I'd never thought to ask her what it was.

NAME'S TED. CAN I HELP YOU WITH YOUR BAGGAGE?

He'd wanted her since he first saw her, in the grocery store produce aisle, examining the cucumbers. The way she turned them over and over again in her hands, the way she held them, and when she snuck one up to her mouth and licked it, he knew he had to have her.

He knew she had a secret. He had one too.

He'd worked in this store for about a year now. Saw tons of these highbrow bitches in their silky braless getups looking at the produce, wishing their husbands fucked them with cocks that big — wishing their husbands fucked them at all — but she was different. She wasn't searching for something she'd lost somewhere under the fluorescent lights. She wasn't desperate for anything like those other rich loose cunts. She knew what she wanted, and he was gonna help her get it.

He watched her for a few weeks, always the same thing — five or six cucumbers, a few zucchini — and she always bought the biggest thickest ones. Week number four, he left a note pinned to one of them for her: SALAD DRESSING IS IN AISLE FIVE. SEE ANYTHING YOU LIKE, THEN CALL ME. He left his cell phone number on the back of a coupon for free douche. While he was writing it, he thought about lifting up that silk dress, ripping her lace undies off, and shoving one of those cucumbers into her on the checkout counter while everyone watched.

He knew he was a lot younger than she was, hoped

she didn't care, and was worried whether or not his apartment was clean when she came up behind him. She whispered, "Creamy Italian," into his ear as she grabbed a bottle off the shelf. She was already half way back down the aisle before he got the guts up to turn around. She wasn't exactly Miss Right, but with that wiggle, she could be Miss Right Now. Her silk dress swished around her bare legs like a whisper in the wind, and he could smell her musk mixed with the perfume she'd sprayed in her panties that morning.

He didn't think she would call, but she did, and his apartment was clean.

A little licorice flavored sterno and a bit of makeshift chemistry relaxed her bitchy mouth enough that a scream wasn't even remotely possible. An hour in and she could hardly breathe, couldn't even moan as he punished her for wanting what she wanted, but it didn't matter. He loved her, and it would hurt so good once he was inside her. He liked hurting her. He knew she wanted to cry out, wanted to bite at him but couldn't. All she could do was reach for him; try to scratch at him, her nails running jagged frantic lines in the sweaty night air around them. He liked it rough, and so did she. He could feel the end coming, the violence building. She kept it hidden from everyone, but he knew she wanted him to feel it: her intestines shot through with fear. She'd wanted this from the start.

She was a Dirty Bitch! He yelled it couple of times, not loud enough to rise above the music playing on the stereo, but loud enough he could feel it burn in his lungs.

She liked it – when he called her names. She said she felt her heart explode every time, said she felt her blood rushing faster inside her. No one could hear her say these things, but she did – say them – with her mouth and with her wide white eyes. "Tell me again," she begged through a breath that was so distant, he thought she had evaporated into herself. It didn't matter what he said in reply. Never did. Not to her, not to any of them. He could tell them he hated them their privilege, loved them their stupidity and their selfishness, but the words didn't matter. Just his voice alone made them tremble. He'd draw blood ... from anywhere he could feel skin, even if it was his own. He'd make that sacrifice for her; show her what they could be together in infinite particles of faith.

There was this yearning he had once, as child. They were both children, both virgins, but she, his first, she had it too: this glistening impenetrable oil slick of a yearning that had soaked through his soul. He'd thought then that it was just a silly youthful yearning. A yearning for entrails, perfumed baubles, and wealth. Like a little girl's wish for a wedding dress. Just a lavender scented daydream, blushed gently across a boy's dimpled cheeks. He had felt ashamed after the first. What a mess he'd made of her.

Now he laughed at the memory, laughed at how indecisive he had been then. "Nasty fucking slut! Fucking cock whore!" He had to stop loving her, just like he'd have to stop loving this one now, but his words just made him all the more insane for her meat, which he had always craved from the first time he had seen her roaming the produce aisle, desperate for a life different than the one she had. Now that she was empty, he could crawl inside her; fill the botoxed void between her flesh and her bones. She said she never wanted him to pull out, but he liked to pull it out. All the way out, and tease the burnished flesh with it until they all begged for more. He stabbed back into her. Once. Twice. Her liver slipped out, slapped against the rotted floorboards. When she cried MORE, he slowed down a little, and then he struck her, the sudden painful stinging sensation sent her bucking against the table.

He smiled.

And she screamed...

A wet gurgling scream before she went limp and silent. She was getting cold. Everything was getting cold. He brought his hands down on her again, waiting for the fire to burn through his palms, as if he had poured lighter fluid on her and lit her the fuck up. He'd tossed that idea around a few times — they get so cold so fast — but he knew it would be completely impossible for him to endure. Besides, all those damn burn marks would never go away. He had such a gorgeous face, and women loved to kiss it. He'd never get any more dates like this if he looked like a leper. He tried once, ended up burning his pecker off. He didn't mind so much though: it was small, an imperfection. Useless. They all have imperfections, and there was more than one way to satisfy the unsatisfied, so he put the flames out of his mind and resumed the cutting and thrusting. She was close to being ready for him, so close he wanted to get naked and slip into her right then, hoping she would swallow him up.

Not yet! Not yet, not yet, not yet...

He grabbed her hair and pulled hard, her head

yanking back, her mouth hanging open in a silent shriek of orgasmic fury. He felt her violent lust for him outside and in, steel on bone, smashing deep into her soul. She had wanted him, couldn't get enough of him, his lips on her mouth, his fingers around her throat, the cherry red glow of seduction glistening on her pubic hair in the streetlight coming through the window. She had wanted him to take her, take her so deep and so dark that she would never dream of another. She wanted to be his. "Fucking whore!" She was his. His knees went weak at the thought.

"This one's a keeper," squawked Esmeralda from off in a shadowed corner of the room.

"But was she?" he asked the parrot in reply. She did have pretty eyes.

"Pretty Eyes, Pretty Eyes, Squawk!" Not fake, like all the bits he'd cut out of her and tossed to the floor.

Maybe he would keep her. He stopped cutting and thrusting and tearing, held his hands in her hot flesh as deep as he could, touched her heart. It was still throbbing against her warm wet flesh.

Yes. Maybe he would keep her.

She was his red-hot bitch, and she'd done everything — JUST — RIGHT — just like she'd said she would when she was pleading for her life.

SCOOP OF CLOTTED CREAM WITH BUGS

In an open grave, he piled his leftovers on top of one another, according to skin color and hairstyle. Five and then three and then five. It'd been quick, each and every one of them. Bam! with a bullet, several to be exact. Sometimes he used a rusty old lawnmower blade, and sometimes he just used his bare hands, but this time ... this time he hammered his love and faithfulness into her skull one adoring stroke of pure rebar steel after another.

An owl sat still on the streetlight just outside the window, watching his feckless temper tantrum mature into justified hatred and rage as the light of the moon meandered across the wet cobblestone driveway. He hoped the damn bird would shit on her sports car.

Yeah, they'd argued.

She called it a chat while she pranced around the room like a gypsy peacock all double entendres and accusations. He didn't like her smell anymore — some fancy expensive French shit she shoved up her cunt every day — and now he was going to crack her fucking skull open and eat her hairy, beige brain. She was tainted like all the others. Full of herself. He didn't think so at first, when he kissed her and she didn't scream, but then a month or so into it, she started talking back, acting above it all. He just wanted things on equal terms.

What's so bad about that?

Why does someone have to be smarter, or more good looking, or more successful than another? Maybe it was him. Maybe he was getting a little more out of it each time. Getting a little better than himself, more disciplined, less eager.

He looked at himself in the mirror, liked what he saw. He was definitely gaining weight; that was for sure.

FRACTURED RADIANT

In all the medical reports, we'd called it a STATE OF PARTIAL DARKNESS. How long had it been? Sixteen hours, twenty-four since exposure. I felt barely visible. I felt feverish, and I could recall a certain noxious odor flirting with the back of my throat.

"It lives in the meat, starved and sexless."

That was all the text message said this time. I figured it was someone I knew who'd sent it to me, someone with imagination and skill. A rebel, a fanatic, an accuser, not like the others, the ones who'd wigged out and fled the cubicles when the flies breached the room. It was chaos, all the screaming and gnawing and fat chunks slapping against flat surfaces, but I didn't panic, of course. Not me. I'm less theatrical, more academic. I've always fed on putrification and agony. I was a product of apathy, all formaldehyde and grey slagging skin. I could feel it, just behind my eyes.

THE SPIKE FEEDS THE PAIN...

I knew this from the trials. We'd switched to solar, dosed the bottles too high. There were side effects: gruesome mathematics and irreversible equations.

"It LIVES in the MEAT."

My mouth started to water. I wish they'd stop texting me. I didn't create the problem, and I certainly can't fix it. Nobody can.

Because IT LIVES IN THE MEAT.

The meat off your bones, I will eat.

BEWARE OF DOG

There is a monster living under my stoop. I used to love him once, but now I have had enough. Lately, he's been dragging road kill home and leaving uneaten bits of entrails all over the garden. It was the stench that put me over the edge. I have to kill him ... I know that ... but I don't know how.

It all started in the summer of '79, behind my house in the little cubbyhole the townhouse developers had called a "backyard." I was thirteen; he was fourteen. We would be freshmen in the fall – high school that is. We'd been sweethearts since kindergarten, I think, so when he wanted to show me his thing, I didn't really think anything of it, and when he wanted me to "put my mouth on it" all thoughts left my head.

He'd gone missing on his sixteenth birthday. I told everyone through a hemorrhagic flood of tears and sobs that "he wouldn't have just run away." Not from me. The police found him three months later, naked and starved, lying in a dumpster. He never talked about what had happened to him, but I had overheard his parents arguing one day, and it was said "horrible things had been done to him." Horrible being only one of a thousand words his mother would use to describe those things she could never speak of.

He didn't start killing people until we got to college ... didn't start eating them until after we were married. Mrs. Adrienne Turner, that's me. I'd call him Addy for short, until last week. I had to put a sign up on the lawn last week. We've never even owned a dog.

After he had disappeared, I was more angry than scared. I thought, or wanted to believe, that he had run off to California to become a celebrity, even though I wasn't really sure how exactly one went about doing that. I always imagined him in skinny jeans and a Gucci shirt, white, pressed, accompanied by some sequined bimbo with synthetic boobs. She would be tall and have huge lips and long painted nails, and she would giggle a lot and flip her hair like a porn star. Still, I often dream of being that porn star. I always loved the way he fucked me just after he'd killed someone. All sweat and anger and release. We haven't fucked in over two years now. He smells bad.

I think rat poison might work, but I have to go now. The mailman is coming, and I want to meet him at the gate. We've been through three in the past year. The last was big boned, screamed like a motherfucker when I maced him, and had too much mail to burn discretely.

DOLL HEADS

"That was a really fucked up thing to say," she said while flicking her cigarette ash on my shirtsleeve. "I know it looks like syphilitic testicles in dick cheese sauce, but no one said you had to eat it."

I was talking to Mollie, of course. Morbid Mollie I liked to call her when there wasn't anything sharp nearby. It was Tuesday, black and still and pouring rain. We were at some depression era bar on the north side. Chinatown. She'd picked the place because she knew I hated the way it smelled when it rained – burnt pistachios, wasabi, and raw sewage. She was sitting at the bar, stabbing something nasty with a pair of chopsticks. Sleazy was her middle name. I hated the way she dressed in those Halloween Nun outfits; Nuns who'd obviously had enough fucking the cross in their spare time and were chewing the pews for a good old-fashioned cock in their mouths. You know the type: toxic with a capital infectious fucking "T." I hated her. Hated her warm meat. "How many you got?" I asked about the suspicious burlap sack lying there, seeping a russet yellow liquid at her feet. I hated looking at her fucking feet too. Her toes looked like a deadly mutant outbreak of knuckles and flesh and hair, all jacked up and crammed into a pair of steel stilettos. I was starting to sweat. Good thing the bartender came by and asked me if I needed something stronger. I did, but even then, I could still taste the vomit and match light residue in the back of my throat. I was hungry. I needed to eat. Fresh or Frozen, I didn't care. Mollie had what I needed ... in the bag at her feet. My plan was to be direct. Cool. Calm. Direct.

"Whatcha got in the bag, Mollie?" I asked again, but she still didn't answer, not yet. Her cigarette smoke danced around my words, and I just stared at the veins in her sagging breasts. I wouldn't have enough money. I knew that, she knew that, but I was hungry. Snap off the head and suck out the juice. That warm delicious juice. They only taste that good when their young, fresh, but I'd settle. These were probably old and stale – rotted biohazard – from the free clinic down the block. I didn't even have enough to pay for that even, but we always came to an arrangement. I'd pay for her dinner, and then I'd have to eat her out. She never said a word. She just smiled at me, stood up, grabbed the bloody bag, and headed for the alley.

DEBT COLLECTORS

I'd taken about a hundred hits before my center gave way like blubber piled on a shit-stained mattress. I'd done the couch surfing dream sex thing to my father's porno mags; the bed-wetting thing, hunkered down against my mother's incessant prayers, which she thought would save my soul; hell, I even dragged in a few shaved cats when I was in college. Ma said I was blessed by the Devil, so blessed, I've had all the cancer therapy a person can stand before they start to feel suicidal. So here I sit, toking it up until I can hear my own voice echoing off the back of my head. A baseball game is being called out in earnest on the radio when the streetlights start to flicker. I don't notice right away because I'm sat here thinking about whether or not I had already put fresh brick dust across all the open doorways. "Dusk to dawn, dust them gone." Ma said that. Said the shadows were on the move. I can remember running down this very street as a kid, trying to hit the porch step before my pop came out and grounded me for being out after dark. "It's a simple thing," he used to say while running his fingers over his belt buckle. He'd had a metal plate in his head for a while, but the government replaced it with plastic. That's why I had to be inside before the streetlights came on. Before the shadows. Those lights were the only warning, Pop said, because he'd lost radio reception on account of the plastic, you see. He'd fought in THE WAR. Never said which one, never said he was afraid. Sometimes I thought he was still fighting it. He'd wring his hands a lot, and I heard him tell Ma once that he felt unclean. When he wasn't in the basement, he was on the porch. He'd sit and listen to the static on the radio for hours, his eyes focused hard on the dark just beyond the porch rail. He'd point every once and a while and say, "Look there boy!" and I would look, squint my eyes, but I wouldn't see anything even though I said that I had. "BASTARDS!" he called them. "Fascist F.A.G. f@!#ing ni@#!rs," he'd say while chucking rocks into the darkness, and I thought his anger seemed kind of personal even though I didn't know what any of those words meant at the time. Now that I think about it, between the layers of smoke and the equally vague layers of pain, maybe it was personal — for him. Maybe those shadows weren't for me to see.

Pop didn't make it home one night before dark. He never came home. Ma blamed the shadows, and I didn't see them when they came for her either.

So now I sit here on this miserable-excuse-shanty-shack hunk of termite shit porch, nothing left of me but blanched skin. Ma's gone. Pop's gone. All I've got left is this dilapi-shack, Pop's hate, and that damn dirty basement. I take another toke on my cigarette and exhale just as the streetlights snap on. I know they're coming, can feel a tightening in my chest, so I reach down and turn the knob on the radio until I'm tuned into the static. Then I stare into the dark just beyond the porch rail …

I stare, and I stare, and I stare until I scream.

UNEXPECTED GUESTS

"I can't get it to stop," my girl said softly, her hands clenching flesh, cartilage, and bone, and I just looked away, said nothing as the night silently slipped through her fingers.

I wanted to say something, but this time, the disappointment kept me silent. This time, I'd lost my nerve to finish it. I don't know why. We'd danced this dance before, me and my girl. This time was no different. We saw the doorknob turn, heard the keys drop, saw the shuffling struggle to find them in the meager light streaming in under the door. They were drunk – Debbie and Dallas – pumped up on ecstasy, strobe lights, and a back alley blowjob. No, this time wasn't a rare occasion. We'd watched them from a virtual distance for some time. We'd lived vicariously through their tales of torture and slavery. We hated them their listlessness, and pitied them their bedroom boredom. We'd watched them slide into dreams and the rotted sewer that is middleclass dementia. We'd even cheered for their hokey homemade porn: the way he knocked her senseless and the way she didn't care as long as her prescriptions got filled. Yes, we'd targeted them. They were careless.

But this night wasn't like all the others.

I remember my knees aching. No padding. Cheap carpet. It was a setup: bingo, AM radio, coconut daiquiris, and their even cheaper looking implants and painted on smiles. Though Debbie's melted right off her pasty face as soon as she saw us. As soon as she knew why we were really there.

"We've never done anything like this before," said the husband when he'd answered our personal ad: Debbie and Dallas seeking a thrill. Ha! They all say that ... and they all regret it after we've finished with them. This time the husband went too far. Poor Dallas. He'd lied a little. Liked it a little more than we had anticipated. He screamed. He pled for mercy. Eventually, he wept. That just turned my girl on more. The love of my life. She couldn't help herself. The smell of sweat and old leather mixed with hatred and fear. "Just a little nick," she'd said, so she could see what he was made of, and then poor Dallas stopped breathing.

"I can't get it to stop," my girl said again, more demanding. We hadn't even done Debbie yet. I wanted to, but she was getting cold, and now we had to clean blood out of the carpet.

PERSIAN CAT

You were on a New York subway train in the middle of the night...

It stank of sweat and urine, scattered newspapers stuck to the floor as a field of lilies in fuchsia flew past us off in the periphery.

You could hear Pan skipping along the roof of the rail car, his hooves trot trot trotting as they tinned and plinked off the steel, idle dreams flitting away in the whirlwind of jolly notes from his flute.

He played that song for a near-sighted girl, spilt milk dripping down her leg as she needfully explored the barren landscape that was her own flesh.

She smiled at you — I smiled at you — and you, in the flickering fluorescent light, smiled back.

ALICEBLUE

"Don't get blood on the apron," she said, but it was too late, the red running like watercolor through the damp fabric.

She often stalked the shadows like this, alone and fitful, weeping white jasmine in the dark hours of the night. I met her here, on the beach. Desired to kiss her in the cold grey rain. She was frail and vulnerable then, tangled up in fishing line and dreams. I wanted her, wanted her to lie down with me in the sand and broken shells. I wanted her to die with me under that drizzling moonlit sky, but I could never say those words. Oh, I said them to others, in passing, in the dark before they knew I was there, but never to her. It was a secret between us, and silence is a virtue, one that can lay no claims to love.

THE KITCHEN SINK

It was a Sunday morning, the day that the levee failed. Five years of fog harvesting, and I felt like a hacker in a velvet wasteland.

Art and politics are a dangerous mix; loneliness and unqualified praise, a happy suicide. You asked me to pass the salt, and when you reached out to take it, I noticed your hands for the first time in a long time. I'd always liked the way your hands felt on me in the dark, the way they stole from me …

The way they bled me.

You salted your runny eggs and then said, without looking at me, that I could be good without being perfect. You said you liked a little mess. Lord knows I've made my mistakes; I don't even want to talk about the sport leathers or the time the belt buckle damn near ripped your ear off. But now, the screams and grunts of ecstasy sound hollow, and the wide white smiles of happy acknowledgement are nothing more than a smooth veneer, constantly in need of polishing. I've become a caretaker in New York City where everyone dines out. You were dining out: a little Chinese on Wednesdays, Hungarian goulash on Tuesdays, and Pizza night with "the guys" on Friday and Saturday nights. When you left after breakfast that day, you left everything, even your toothbrush, which I had always used to scrub the toilet on Sunday afternoons.

MUSE

"My love tool, baby, it's set to drill and thrill," he said with a smooth oily smile, muscles gleaming in the sultry late afternoon light as the ceiling fan's tattered paddles clapped and flapped, its motor groaning overhead.

She smiled at him because hers was set to bludgeon. Hell, she didn't even mind the cheap motel stink of him. He was rock hard, dangling in front of her like candy cum-coated sin. She wanted him to take her — hard and violent — because she felt violent.

She felt hungry.

She'd felt flushed red and moist for over a year now. It was just a moment, this moment, and that was all she had. A suitcase by the door, a lipstick smeared wine glass cast to the floor — broken — in an array of shattered crystal, shiny and sharp. But everything was perfect now: his wide white smile, his taut skin, the way his tongue kissed a fever into all her soft secret places. Yes, it was perfect, the way he tasted, the way he smelled, and the words he would never say. There could be no other perfect thing in a moment of fear and exhilaration bought and paid for with cold hard cash.

He had no name, and she didn't care as he covered her mouth and slammed himself into her.

He had no shame, and neither did she, the taste of him still wet on her lips as she kissed him.

He felt no guilt or regret, so she envied him as she watched him caress himself while he watched her beg, wanting for more.

It felt dirty.
It felt savage.

And it was worth it, she thought, smiling as she pulled the key silently out of the lock on the front door. The lights were out, the TV still on, a half-finished cigarette still burning away in the ashtray. She wanted to wake him, that man on the sofa who didn't know her anymore. She wanted to wake him and tell him what she'd done, wanted to tell him it was worth it: worth every red cent that had been poked, prodded, cajoled, and licked out of her "tired old cunt."

LESSONS FROM THE GRIDIRON VOYEURISM AND GINGIVITIS

I'd made it all up, and I'd failed miserably. The story of my life, that is. It's all in the details, and I was never very good at details, even on-line. The syntax was off, as it always was for me. It's a perfectionist's burden, you see, but we decided to meet anyway. She ordered the steak – rare, bloody – which was unusual for her, she said, and she ate it with her hands, pausing only to sip her Chianti and cola from a straw. It was a classy place, and she was a classy chic.

"Mind pissing into this?" I asked her after she announced that she needed to go powder her nose.

I'd just put it out there, come what may. She took the plastic cup and shot me a meaty smile in reply.

What? It's sex in the age of potato chips and mad flight attendants: there's tortured bodies, accusations, and a ton of wreckage. Yeah, back in the day, I used to be a crusader for peace and free love, a lone idiot savant. Back then it was all dark rooms and back-alley peep shows. It wasn't the sort of deliverance you'd get with a snake charming kootch like this chic, but generally a memorable first and last date nonetheless.

She sat back down, that red dress sliding halfway up from the netherworld to eternity. I smiled back and said nothing to which she responded by pouring the liquid she had collected into my glass and subsequently squeezing a lemon into it while stirring the ice.

"So what's yours?" she asked, but I wasn't sure what mine would be just yet.

We're talking about words here, of course – safe words – not the sort of illiterate monosyllabic poetry that makes you cringe during a blood draw, but the kind we all use to seek clemency in the middle of the night from time to time ... like a crucified kiss.

She whispered me hers, and at that moment, I knew I wouldn't need one.

MORATORIUM

The sky had shifted to grey, the storm past as the moon descended on the horizon. "No words," he whispered. Just breath coated in salt and sweat: skin on skin on sand, grinding cock moans deep and guttural. Fists clenched. Feet dug in. Knees ragged and bruised on sharp shells. Their mouths wet, their hair ... wet with inky blue stardust and the spray of the tide.

She said, "I hate you," and he smiled. Teeth sharp. Kiss penetrating her vital organs, and the tide came in, again, washing over her back as she transcended him, his cock a steel shaft, rusted in the moonlight. It looked red, like a worn blade, even in the dark as the earth moved away beneath them.

"No words," he said again, his hands in her hair, on her hips – rough and persistent – in the small of her back and on her throat.

She said, "I hate you," once more, but the air was thin, thinning, thinner, than she needed it to be as the stars faded away along with her memory of him, inside her. His thrust, his warmth, his hatred, too, she'd wanted once as he replied in kind before she slipped back and away with the tide.

PROVINCIAL LOVE AND ETHER

The goddamn telephone was always ringing. No one I know would call me at this hour ... any hour. No one I know would call me here, period. I felt like a ragtime prohibition floozy with one foot in a drain and the other atop a case of Chinese gunpowder, all blanched almond cheeks, dental dams, and laughing gas.

"What's so funny?" you asked when I giggled wildly at the thought of someone else and that they might be calling you. You couldn't know what I was thinking, though, and I shouldn't have found it amusing, since I wasn't the one playing with all the sharp objects: You were, and I loved to hate you, even if you didn't notice or didn't care. You just wanted me to "hold still" as you leaned in close, the moisture vapor collecting in tiny droplets on the inside of your mask.

INTERN

Six, seven, ten, with a snap and a pop, she crossed and uncrossed her legs as she cracked her gum into the telephone receiver with complete and utter disdain for the customers on the other end of the line. Gotta love interns, their youthful defiance and their blatant disregard for rules, regulations, and even the most basic HR guidelines.

She was Alice, and she was a tease. We'd been exchanging sexy notes across the aisle for a couple of months now. She wrote shit I could never imagine in all my wildest wet dreams. Sometimes I had to use the private bathroom stall or run out to my own car in the parking lot at lunch to jack off because she got me so hot all the goddamned time. She was pulp pornography in leather skirts and big girl heels that were way too high for her to navigate. She teetered on them, licking her lips like she was standing atop a tart cherry lollypop. Her bare skin candy-coated glistening sweetness.

She'd record voice mails for me, put post-its under my keyboard, and leave lipstick smeared napkins on my chair when I went to get coffee. She wrote such god-awful dirty things on slivers of used notepaper, left over Thai takeaway menus, and the waxed papers that come off the back of maxi pads.

I pictured her sitting in my lap, facing me, her legs over the arms of the chair ... SHIT, MY PHONE'S RINGING ... it's late, and the cleaning lady is just two cubes over. I cover Alice's mouth so she can't scream out. She wants it hard. She wants it rough. She moans against the palm of my hand and shoves her pert little twenty something lacy tits right into my face so I can suck at them through the red silk while she slams herself against me, her hips grinding against mine like a greasy machine head.

She wrote to me in passing once that she loved the way I wanted to fuck her, in the dark, just the glow of the computer screen lighting the sweat on her skin. My pants down around my ankles, her panties hanging over the side of the trash can. I laughed because she thought that I wouldn't be able to get her bra off, but I loved the red lace, so I'd just pull it aside, the underwire scraping against my chest. She'd have those killer heels on, too … and a pen in her hair. I imagined she'd get her hands all tangled up in my hair, her elbows on my shoulders as she rocked back and forth against me.

She was such a horny bitch. I wanted it, wanted her so bad. I want to lick and suck and bite at her ... the sweat falling onto the paper. "Don't fucking stop, you fucking bitch office whore," I'd cry out, and then I would feel it — warm and hot — slipping out of her, before she'd collapse, trembling in my arms.

I put the wet piece of paper down and grabbed my crotch with both hands. Good thing it's late. I'd blasted my load all over my self. I stood up to pick the wet wedge out of my ass when I heard a sigh a few cubicles down. The goddamn cleaning lady's been in the next cube the whole time — jacking it to me jacking it. I felt my face get hot, so I zipped up real quick and began to crumple the notepaper when I noticed there was writing on the back. It was from Alice, and all it said was "Bet that broom handle is awful stinky now."

GHOSTS IN WINTER

My mouth on yours, like an open wound.
My hands on your face,
My hair falling softly against your skin.

Your cock was hard against my hip as our legs tangled together with our whispered words. Words like want, and hungry, and desperate needful love. "Just touch me ... don't fuck me," I said to you. "Let me feel the sinew in your flesh," and your hands slipped into the small of my back. You wanted to feel my lust, your own lust, like you always did, but "I don't want to feel my lust right now ... I just want to feel you." My hands like the feel of you ... the gentle arc of your abdomen and the tight little snarl of pubic hair you keep trimmed just for me. I touch your hipbone ever so slightly with the back of my hand and take your bottom lip into my mouth...

"Don't look at me," while I adore the you that is your flesh. "It makes me feel starving and weak." You laugh at me, and I apologize for waxing poetic because it's a different kind of hunger that consumes me today. A hunger I'd forgotten to appreciate along with the miles of distance in your flesh that I had always overlooked in my haste.

I want to know that distance.

I want to know the way you breathe, the way you die just a little when you sleep, and the way your hair falls against your forehead when you rise up in ecstasy above me. I want to know what your heart and your liver and your kidneys taste like fresh and warm while your heart is still pumping, and I want to know what the palms of your hands feel like against my cheek when they are slick with blood and bile. I want you to put your fingers in my mouth. I want to taste you on them, knowing that you were thinking of me when you took the blade and caressed yourself into oblivion.

It's not your cock I want today or your desperate needful love. The want is deeper today, darker, like the copper smell on your breath when you lie to me like you mean no harm when you say the word "FUCK."

You say I make you feel wicked. You ARE, wicked, when you worship the flesh of a whore, your hands on my throat when you say it, and then you make me believe it long enough to deny it. You want me to deny it, to deny you, to pretend I could survive YOU long enough to drain you from my veins. But I can't ... deny you. Deny what I am.

"Don't fuck me," I say again softly into your ear as I wrap my legs around your trembling waist. I just want to press myself into you, until there is nothing left, like the white bones of a ghost, lost and longing, lamenting the transparency of its own flesh.

PARKED CARS

When she met him, it was as if she'd stepped on a perfect piece of glass. Ground it into her heel and exhaled a breath of perfect pain. It was a mistake, her love for him. Bad geography. A desert. A lost highway set ablaze by a gasoline fire and bald tires. She'd used the nip-slip, caught him off guard, and so he pulled over. "What's a freaky young thing like you doing way out here in Death Valley?" he asked, and she responded with a flick of her hair.

"So this is Death Valley, huh?" She popped her gum a few times and leaned her trussed up cleavage in closer. "Where are all the bodies then?"

He laughed with his shoulders then pushed the passenger door open for her. Regrettable, she thought as she slid across the leather towards him. He had a pair of steel scissors hanging from the rearview mirror and the stink of cheap chardonnay on his breath.

"I like your tattoos," he said as he rattled the keys in the ignition, "And yes, I'm married. Do you care?"

She didn't.

She was a cutter, and she didn't care about anything unless it hurt her. Maybe he would. He had that look about him. The footnotes of existence had creased and leathered his face. She wanted to touch the lines, lick the salt from his lips. "You're super cute," he said. Said she'd got swank, but his voice was rough and muddled, and she heard the word SKANK. That's when she fell in love with him. He knew it too and guiltily stroked her leg into a budding rouge, exacting his pleasure from the small measures of skin he could imagine with his fingertips.

She let him.

She saw within his eyes the distillation of an unfinished masterpiece for years he had only envisioned in his mind. Nothing could separate her from him in that moment.

No, nothing ever would.

Their love would run together, and eventually, when it came, would trickle away with the rain.

She drove very far that afternoon. Far and Fast. His car was much faster than her old Pontiac piece of junk. She liked the wind in her hair too, and the way the fractured windscreen toyed with the lines on the road in the midday sun until the road was nothing more than an idea, a masterpiece of chaos, rippling in the desert heat.

WD-FORTY

Sing me an organ grinder's taxi ride gospel and let the tide coast in," she said. That was her way of saying, "poor you," when I started whining about how emasculating our relationship was. She had this fixation for white orchids and pain and a shotgun barrel of whiskey a day.

We hadn't spoken in a while.

She said she missed me but couldn't tell me why.

She'd invited me to dinner, expected me to look her in the eyes, but the sparks coming from the belt sander were a distraction. We'd had this conversation before. She said if I wanted to be her muse, "then I'd better just shut the hell up," but the straps were too tight, the stilettos too high. They made my legs look bowed like a cowboy who'd taken one too many rough rides. "You're a rough ride," she said through the side of her mouth as she lit one of them long brown European cigarettes she liked so much. She said she liked how they looked in her hand and between her lips when she watched herself smoke in the mirror.

She liked the taste of the tobacco.

I didn't like it. It left little dirty bits on my tongue when she kissed me. She rarely kisses me these days. She said she wasn't interested in that anymore, that for some reason, the number thirteen bothered her, haunted her like a lounge lizard with a caterpillar smile. She said, "I loved you once, when you were fearless," but I'm not anymore, apparently, so she put out her smoke and went back to buffing and oiling the rusted hinges she'd always said were mine.

CHROME BUMPERS

I could feel my whole body clench when she walked into the room wearing nothing but a clear plastic rain slicker, a pair of my white briefs, and red rubber boots. She said she liked to do it in the rain with the lightning lighting up her face.

It was late, pouring outside, and I had already taken care of business to a six-pack and some porn. She must have heard me, wanted some of that action, but I didn't think I had it in me until she bent over to turn off the TV. Her nipples pressed hard against the plastic.

I said, "No," so she went and got the keys to my beat up old pickup truck.

"I can't see shit," I said as I twisted the steering wheel, the road blurred in the rain ahead of me as we bucked, swerved, and weaved our way down the dead end road to the quarry on the outside of town. She had her head out the window. Screamed. Delight. Rain kissing crystalline to her eyelashes, her hair pressed close to her lips.

She said all kinds of dirty things to me, and she smiled when she said it, but I said, "No," and kept on driving.

She liked the ledges, where the rock was loose and slippery. The rain slicker flashed in the headlights as she danced to *Frankie Goes to Hollywood*, blasting from the car stereo. I loved the way the sludge hit her bare thighs every time she smacked her heels into the soft earth. I lit a smoke, watched her, thought about her pressed wet to the filthy hood of my truck.

"I want you," she said. "Want to feel you next to me, on me, in me."

I said, "No." Then I kissed her mouth while she fumbled with my jeans, pushed them down to my knees with her feet. The engine was steaming, and the rain felt good on my ass. I flipped her over, pressed her face into the metal, her nails scratching into the fading paint. She said she loved me, but she didn't really love me. She loved a good time. I just happened to be in the right place at the wrong time. I pushed the rain slicker up to her shoulders, grabbed her hips. Her rubber boots squeaked as she struggled against the bumper. Her lips were wet. Her words were wet. Her lies slick with sweat. She said I was a bastard, a motherfuckin' tease, so I put a rag in her mouth to shut her up.

And the rain came down, pressed the night in close around us.

She was the tease. She wanted it. I wanted it too, I guess. But she always said, "No."

On the way home, she said I tasted like gas and lithium grease, and "According to the news," she said, it was gonna rain all week.

ACAPULCO IN WINTER

She wore red chemical gloves when we made love. The ones she stole from the nuclear power plant where she worked.

I often imagined that they had come into contact with radioactive material and that as she caressed me, I would grow to mutant size. She would just smile when I said it out loud. I didn't satisfy her the way I always wanted to, but she didn't seem to mind.

Our relationship, well, it was a missed connection, a series of straight rocket slices of pain to the backs of your eyelids. An honest struggle with death, and the rain came down. Didn't hurt much, not anymore. She said the longer I kept going with it the more comfortable I would start to feel with the metaphor and how its seemingly irrelevant questions about low voltage and darkness and the brisk drizzle of spring rain against the plywood universe might change my mind about how I juiced myself up.

"Me," I pointed to the scar in the middle of my chest when I said it, "You know I prefer a light tap in the vein." The kind that leaves your teeth dry. Snap. Pop. Redline express all the way to heaven and back, baby. "Betcha miss me when I'm gone."

She said she didn't, but I've touched it, you see — the GOD particle — refracted the distance between the layers of my skin. She said I couldn't do it. Said I was too retro and that I should rent a time-share, stay for less.

I hated it when she called herself cheap.

WATER COOLER NU ALLONGE

I loved her like a paper cut — my Jenny — all sunshine and red leather smirks, that girl of mine, bridled at the bottom of a ravine like a showroom mannequin doused in gasoline and the stench of roller-coaster fear and vomit. She was a white-hot hellcat, blessed top to bottom.

She sat in the cubicle next to mine — skin as pale and creamy as a manila envelope — and she sat there day after day decapitating political figures on her photo-editing program to pass the idle time between getting coffee and typing reports. She wore skirts: silk, and lace, and in the winter, black and red checked flannel with fringe at the slit. She was always fingering her garters when she thought no one was looking.

I was looking. I was always looking.

When she walked to the water cooler she was like a floor show at one of those Can-can clubs — swish, and legs, and perfumed panties. I imagined the warmth between her legs and how her lips would feel on mine. I imagined that she would like a dry martini if I made her one, and I imagined that she liked cats and colored lights and tinsel on her Christmas tree.

I wondered if she even noticed me at all, and often I imagined that she did.

She never took a single sick day, so how could she not notice me and how I ached for her, how I wanted inside her.

Her boss was a dick, always touching her with his fat fried-onion fingers while he rubbed his crotch into the back of her chair. It didn't make her feel sexy. It made her feel sad. She put binder clips on her fingers until her nails turned blue, and she scribbled her sadness down on the menus of all the local suicide buffets. That's how I got to know her – in the margins of a trashed menu where extra grease made everything more meaningful. She'd only ever smiled at me once, when I came around the corner near the fire exit and caught her ducking into the janitor's closet for a smoke. I started meeting her there, and we'd sit in the dark, in silence, listening to each other inhale and exhale as we gave up our dreams ... seven minutes at a time.

FLASHCARD FREESTYLE AND THAT WICKED, WICKED BANDWIDTH

Before the killer cheeseburgers and sex toys, I was a free man, listening to my own love dirge in the wee dark hours with fatal abandon. Then it all caved in around me: crystal wine glasses, decadent desserts, and dirty pool water. That's how these things happen in the real world. It's a party — no extra legroom and the incandescent lighting's a little weak.

Glen, my best friend, wanted revenge, domination in a single drop of sweat. She'd never been his girlfriend. She had hits in the millions. She was a ghost, a construct, bountiful acres of flesh he hadn't had the sense to manhandle the way he'd wanted to. He said she was ugly, pixilated, but I didn't think so. She had small hands and big dreams. Now she was my baby strange pushing the hard edge in the periphery. Our romance was a brief and righteous act of lust and longing, not a snot-palmed-purplish song of internet dating desperation, I can tell you that.

She was mine, in real life.

I was in the back of the room; she at the bar, and I watched her squeezebox a penny in those lacy little capris with her ankles bare and her warm lips crusin' the cocktail rind at ten seconds to midnight. Five, four, three, two, one ... She didn't kiss anyone, so I texted her site, hoping she was still mine.

RANCID DUSK

I hate shopping for gifts: Christmas, birthdays, fucking Valentine's day. It all sucks. The dollar store was the best thing ever invented after edible underwear and chloroform. Someone said people hate as they love. Well, I hate loving you. It's unreasonable rhetoric. Who the hell has a three-week anniversary? Even the sex hasn't lost its apple pie-puppy-shine yet, so why call in the paramedics with this anniversary shit, you brainwashed halfway-house bitch; now just hold still.

Sorry. I didn't mean to yell at you. It's just that ... I'm a hostage, living away the thrilling minutes of a death-room romance with listeria licking at my crotch.

What's wrong with you?

Was it the rusty chainsaw? The way I said "please" like I actually meant it?

We'll I did mean it. It was dark. You were so lovely and lost, waiting at the train station all silk and lace and soft skin, and I'd had too much to drink.

Your legs look so hot in those leather straps. You weren't sure if they would, but they do.

Please now, just sit still. No one knows what will make them happy. I certainly don't. Your tits, your mouth, your ass? Maybe. We've only known each other for three weeks. What difference does it make whose panties those are? Oh come on, don't cry. You know I hate it when you cry.

I know, I know ... they make you jealous, the way they just glare at you over the picket fence. Their sexy gaping mouths and swollen tongues, eyes like wet charcoal.

No, they're not sneering at you, darling. Why would you think that? They mean nothing to me. Sure, they wanted me. They all want me, but three weeks is a long time, baby. More than I gave any of them.

Yes, you're special, of course you are, and I know what I said, but look, I polished the pike all nice and shiny for you. Sanded the rust off and everything.

It'll look nice with your earrings, if you'd just ... hold ... still.

WHAT SWEET MUSIC THEY MAKE

That day I enthusiastically wasted on paper lanterns and the sharp wooden stares of sugar and flesh. She was pale with deceit, a product of meddling and worm-eaten explanations and grandstanding. "It meant nothing to me," she said, and I sneezed the exhaust that was her from my lungs. She had perfumed hair. They all did, those who honored and obeyed, and those who couldn't be bothered. The phone rang. She reached for it – clumsy – and it landed at my feet. "Telemarketer," she claimed, and I felt my hand grow tighter around the handle. I was always wildly excited by the little things: the weight of tools in my hand, the gentle run of the wind against frozen eyelids in the moonlight, the crimson against dry lips and gritted teeth, and then the stiff drink after, tainted by lipstick at the rim. She was all sorry and so forth, keeping a casual distance, and then she bared her breasts at me, giggled, told me to take one for the wedding album before she threw her engagement ring into the heap of soiled clothes I'd left to soak in the sink with last night's dirty dishes.

Valentine's Day. A Spring Slaughter.

I thrust some Kleenex into my pocket, grabbed a Coca Cola, and headed for the door. I'd called her my little spring lamb, and she called me "corny" just as my hand was reaching for the doorknob. I unlatched the deadbolt and pulled. The cold gusted in, and I could hear it: a whispering, a crawling skittle of cockroach legs and eyes wide open, crying in the dark. They were always whispering, sometimes in cadence with the dripping rain, plink, plink, plinking off the tin roof some ways away in the distance, sometimes like a white kiss carried upon a thistle flower, swaying with ice and snow, but they were always whispering – demanding – almost in silence, to hear the voice of God over the melancholy braying of the other lambs.

RELAPSE

I love the way you smell, the way you taste of sweat and leather, and I love the way your hands feel on my body, the way they take me, the way they bleed me. I love the way the blood hits the wall and splatters like cooking grease as the whip bears down against the soft ivory flesh of my back.

Again comes the pain,

And then harder,

And then again.

There is no humility in it. No sin. No salvation, and no acquittal. I am an addict. Had written it twelve times in that blood on the wall.

Addict, addict, addict...

Addicted to the pain, addicted to the shame, addicted to all the whitewashed tears that fell like clots of blood upon the paper when there were no more lonely words to write in the darkness.

I love you, the way your flesh rots my soul, the way your bones waste me. I love your shadow, and the gravestone you took me on the very first time we met.

CONTEMPLATIONS ON A ROMANCE

She slaps me and then tries to run away. Tries to. There's light snow approaching on the horizon, a pinkish hue that will eventually erupt into a fury of ice and wind. I can see the cabin from the gazebo, can see the orange glow of the fire through the window on the North side.

She had said she wanted to come here. "How romantic," she'd said with a giggle. But now she's just shaking — from the cold.

We'd had an argument the other day. A riot of hurtful and heinous words erupting from mouths rinsed with red wine and sighs.

No sexualized violence.

No gnashing of teeth.

No overburdened thrusts of diminished temper, like the cheeky stuff those erotic novels are made of.

It was an argument.

Plain and simple.

Just words.

Brambles and thorns and blood.

I feel like I don't know her.

And maybe in a way, it's true.

Our problems began early. We're living in a Teflon market, you see, and she says, all the time, that she's allergic to Teflon. She isn't. She's a hypochondriac. That isn't the half of it, though. I hear all the gossip, all that shit they whisper behind my back. I hear that our vital signs are being taken and measured from a distance by prying eyes jittery over their own little deceits. I detest them, those fat wife collectors and their blinged out whores, so firm in faith and body trying to tell me that my idle dreams will eventually become nightmares I will never wake from.

Sure, I'm to blame for my part: my violences are everywhere, and her failings ... so clever. I'm not like them though. I'd walked a mile in those shoes once, all shiny and muscular, but they aren't comfortable. They pinch and press against my arches. That's how I know I'm a ditch-digger — leather bootstraps and old grease on my hands — and as I shovel the frozen soil back into the hole, I know and she knows, whether she likes it or not, that that is all I will ever be.

BEYOND THE WINDOW

You were holding a wilted flower; it was coated in dew. You'd picked it that morning. I knew this because I could see you, beyond the window, as you crept like a thief into the long shadows, singing a sweltering night song in your heart. Your tentative steps linger like a kiss upon my soul. How sweet you were then, quiet and careful, how innocent that springtime moment when the tiled roofs gleamed in the rising sun, moist still from the evening rain. That rain was in your hair. I could smell it that night as I spoon fed you soup from a wooden bowl while we listened to the sound of bombs echoing back on us from the distant hills.

BLOWOUT

Of all the weird places to spend the last night of your life." That's what I was thinking in the tense final moments before I bled out and died. I wasn't thinking "Don't pull over," and I wasn't thinking about the fog or my asthma inhaler or the mummified remains of my boyfriend, which I had only just dug up from my backyard and placed in the trunk of my car. Probably a bad decision, since it's been so scorching hell-fire hot the past couple of days, but that's the thing, I hadn't thought about anything in weeks — years really — except that jughead in the trunk. I'd lost track of the time somewhere around Albuquerque in the 60s. I should have eased off the accelerator, should have known that the heat from the asphalt and the hail of rifle fire would blow out the tires. You'd be surprised how fast the details of your predicament emerge at one-hundred-sixty miles per hour in a shower of shattered glass. I was in over my head; I knew this, but the farther you can go on your own, the better.

INK

You transfix me. Scribble your name on my slate. White Chalk. Black Ink. It's a blood splotch – bloated – so what? "It'll heal," you said, and I thought you were crazy. Or maybe it was the other way around? Your spit tastes of salt ... of raw meat ... and your soul smells sticky, always has, so don't try to tell me it's artistic temperament. It's not. You're just crazy.

You.

Not me.

CRAZY.

Fishhooks and flatbed trucks with greasy wheels. I don't exist in your world. I desired your flesh, once, your death, maybe twice, but you walked out.

Rotten.

A corpse.

A martyr with an emblem of my hatred branded to your chest. Hammered iron and hot coal. You said I was flaky. You said linseed oil isn't a tonic. The roads and fields have vanished from my memories. What's wrong with eating dog meat? Or fighting? Or fucking? Or Sleep? I knew it all along. It was a one-tank trip I needed forever, even though I knew it wasn't possible with you.

BROKEN

The way the moonlight struck her shoulder blades as she sat slumped over the table – face in a pile of blood and vomit – haunts me to this day. Maybe it was because I never trusted her, which was my only defense against the constant betrayals that she inflicted upon me. This was the worst by far. She'd said in her message that this night, the night I found her, would be something special. Something liberating, for the both of us. I was careful not to make any assumptions. She'd always said I assumed too much, expected too much. I think I understand what she meant now. Savage are those unsettling revelations that beg your attention at 2 A.M.

By the time I got there, it was hot in her apartment, stuffy, like the windows hadn't been opened in months. No air. No power. The refrigerator stank so bad from the outside, I didn't want to open it. The roaches swarming the pizza box on the counter were bad enough. Something smelled like eggrolls. Greasy dumpster cabbage. It's all borrowed time, I kept thinking, like yesterday when I pulled her pigtails at recess. We hadn't evolved much from that prepubescent tension. Not even after twenty years. A foggy twenty years of keyholes and sprockets and noisy snare drums. I leaned over and twisted the ribbon in her hair through my fingers. Even the watchers need to be watched, I thought. She'd always watched me, but I guess my eyes had wandered. I poured myself a glass of wine. The bottle was old, warm, and the liquid tasted of lint. I guzzled it down, then sat down, and told her she'd looked better. She always did, by candlelight. I lit a book of matches and tossed the flaming pile of sulfur and cardboard into the ashtray by her left arm, which was blackish blue in the dim light and covered in belt marks.

She'd ordered Chinese takeout. We'd do that sometimes — last night, last week … or maybe it was last year — sit in the candlelight and sip wine. "What kind of life should we have?" she'd always ask with greasy Kung Pao chicken juice on her lips, and I'd sniff the spicy helplessness on her flesh before resuming those innocent caresses I used to placate her so often with. I never answered her. She had a haunting in her eyes that reflected back into you so deeply, it was frightening, so my silence was never spiteful. She'd say, "There's no right or wrong way to feel about it," but the truth of the matter was, I just didn't know if there was any kind of life we could have.

SPANISH LIMES

It was a soft summer night in paradise, flashing crimson words lighting up the smoky gloom of the sidewalk: LIVE, said the one. ALL NUDE, said another. The triple X glow of sex against the curve of a hip and the hard-candy gloss of a garter. Yeah, it was the kind of hazy humid night an insomniac could appreciate by candlelight, but the ice wasn't cold enough in my margarita, and the salt tasted like asphalt. I didn't even know what they were talking about, the two massive blue-black shapes looming in the darkness behind me. I can't even recite the friggin alphabet the normal way.

LITHIUM AND GIN

It's called Death Spank," said an acquaintance of mine as we sat outside in the heavy rain, sipping gin at a local cafe. He'd whispered it like it was some kind of depraved secret, his words followed up with a grin and a YOU'LL LOVE IT. I'M TELLING YOU nod and a wink. He was right. I knew that I would. It was just crazy enough for me: not head in a gas oven crazy, well, maybe a little, but maybe I needed that. Maybe I needed a fall-to-my-death fear crisis or a piss-in-the-face-of-convention moment to wake me out of my coma. I felt boring. All my thoughts had started to stink like carrion in the Sudanese sun. I wasn't really looking for anything in particular, just trying desperately to avoid a manslaughter conviction, if you get my meaning. He got it, of course. He knew where I was at, my acquaintance, that is, and he agreed with a hand gesture followed by an argument on innocence and white lace. "They just want to toy with us and then kill us all slow and domestic like." Turn us into withered old begging cripples. At least that's how I saw it lately. The viewpoint was selfish and unjustified, I know, but if there was some sort of strength in an extra inch, then why not take a yardstick until you're screaming red and raw. At the very least, it had to taste better than the gin.

SCHEDULE C

It was his bare ass in chaps and the way he tossed effortless smiles at people on the street. It was refreshing to see such positive energy being flung, bungee-style, out into the world. It's harder than it sounds, bleeding delirious happiness. I'd seen him before while I was driving my car, while I was sat at the local cafe, and once, behind me, while I was in the elevator going up to the fifth floor. I'd been having a bad day that day. I was grouchy, piss-faced, pantyhose sagging in the crotch. It was interview day, and I just knew I was going to wash up dead in the sweltering heat. I imagined that the whole elevator situation was some satirical vignette – a day in the life of an economic casualty – and the headline would read DUNK TANK VICTIM STALKED BY TATTOOED COWBOY AND TAX SCAMS. I was a big cake kind of person, a future criminal with restless legs and a nice haircut; well, that's how I assumed I would be described in the closing arguments. "Rape is a weapon of war," whispered the Cowboy into my ear as the android supermodel announced our approach to the fourth floor. I was pretty sure he meant "rape" as a metaphor, even through the hot, bleached-out breath he was depositing on my neck in frothing spit bubbles of joy. I stabbed him in the eye with my nail file. Nobody saw that coming, least of all the auditor who was waiting for me on the next floor.

A DISTANT AFTERNOON

They called it hail damage – those sparks you see across your eyelids. At least that's what I think they called it as I lie here with the IV drip, drip, dripping into the vein in my arm, waiting for the final push. Is it in the vein or the artery? I can't tell by looking at them. I can only tell by the blood spatter when I cut them. My Daddy took me out for my first. He said there were always new uses for old things. Old things, he called them. I wasn't sure what he meant by that; I was only twelve at the time, but I later realized, after a twist of fate kept one alive longer than I had planned, I knew that I was seeking something divine, or as my Daddy put it, "Using them to see yourself clearly." That's how it was done, until things got rushed, got blurry. It was a miscalculation. "A mistake nobody but a retard like you would make," my Daddy would have said. You see, he was a cake-eater too, in way. Told me I was a chosen one, despite my being a moron, so there was no sense trying to run away. So I didn't. I had macaroni and cheese and fried chicken for supper last night. They said I could have anything I wanted, and I thought that's what I wanted, but it's churning in my stomach now, so maybe it wasn't. But I would never know, 'cause my Daddy ain't here to tell me so.

IN FLIGHT ENTERTAINMENT

"Go after what you want, with a vengeance," she said through the drainpipe down the backend of a sequined thong as she handed me a small cello package with what looked to be an overcooked corndog in it.

Cell phones, sex assaults, and rudeness. The budget package they called it, complete with dinner and light entertainment. Fly the compromised sky: BLUE TOENAIL AIRLINES. At least the rodents haven't chewed through the fuselage yet. And so it began. It always begins this way, with a chill in the blood. I do this twice a year: dial 911 while I'm packing, ditch the meds, and sweat it out cold in mid-air, but this time, the stewardess won't stop talking. She'd posed nude, run the porn circuit, even got an honorary mention and a small gold-plated trophy in the shape of a cock. She was an emotional eater, a sniff-before-tasting never-take-no-for-an-answer kinda girl. Fitting really. She said recovery was a state of mind, that I was on the right path, and when I looked around, the crowd of passengers was cheering me on. She had one of those silky smooth accents — French maybe — the kind that could deliver authority straight to your groin. She was convincing, and so I took a small labored breath, like it was a favor at my own expense. "Breathe," I told myself. "Just breathe ... and keep staring at that flashing light." The one that told me to keep myself strapped in. I would, of course, gritting my teeth while waiting for the tinkling trolley to come darting past with its absurd collection of tiny little binge vials. Six, seven, ten with or without ice, and then the wheels touch down. It feels like a bomb blast in a subway station, and I can just barely hear myself screaming...

MODUS VIVENDI

I tried not to flinch at the screaming and the echo of gunshots off in the distance. I tried not to stare at the rats picking through the rancid pile of maggot infested garbage on the front porch, either. From the car park, even with binoculars, you don't see any of this. You've got a name, an address, and an order, and that order doesn't come with any pre-conceived notions. Well, maybe it does, but I still tried to be professional as I extended my hand to him. His was bloody from wiping his nose and slapping at the mosquitoes that kept landing on his scabby bald head. I didn't want to hand him the paper, didn't want him to take it from me, either. I always felt bad for some reason, after I met them in person. You see, in my shoes, you're just a piece of paper to serve. You don't know what falsehoods have flourished, who was in control, or who had dragged who through the vomitous mire that had once been a life. You're supposed to look at the floor and just see the floor. I can't remember who said that, but it's true. He was just another OFP — contemptible, pathetic — nothing more, and he smelled like shit and wet-house serenity. He didn't even push back or want to hear the arguments. He just wanted to know "How many feet?" as if that made all the difference in the world ... and maybe it did, to someone other than me.

HYPERTHYROIDISM

There was this diner I liked to go to. A real greasy spoon if you feel the academic need to pigeonhole its culinary style. I liked it there, but I ain't no sweat lodge expert or nothing. I just liked the way it smelled most days and the way the brittle red vinyl stuck to your skin when you were wearing short pants. It was a typical person's joint, except during the summer heat ... and when the moon was full. Last week, the moon was the biggest it had been in years. In the booth next to me, worn out shoes and broken teeth were discussing Rachmaninov and the merits of romanticism and structural ingenuity in Russian classical music while a drone wiped up the spit and blood that had collected on every surface around them. Then there was this slovenly waitress. I called her Tuesday 'cause that seemed to be the only day she worked. She had huge breasts with light red peach fuzz all over them, and she covered them with divisive little bits of flare. She often burned the coffee, but I didn't mind. In every bitter cup there lay at the bottom — like the grit in Juan Valdez's soiled underpants — her dreams of the Jamaican coastline. She was no sommelier, but she could sure pour a cup of joe, and her eyes, she had the eyes of divine retribution. She told me once that I didn't need the fake iodide ... and you know what, she was no naked bicycle ride with Gandhi, but I believed her.

A WALK DOWN AVENUE DES CHAMPS-ELYSEES

The air smelled of saffron crushed under foot, the clouds of white smoke and jungle prayer, filling the empty spaces as the sun dripped heat down the sides of your opium pipe. At dawn, you might venture into the street like a spider creaking out from a crack in the folds of time. You might visit a cafe and pass the morn idly by. Later, you might dance, sure-footed, along the wet cobbles only to find yourself at the market. You might even trade some spice for a cupful of soiled leaves, or bestow a kind word upon a stranger – a stranger whose sad siren song made you think of the postman three days past, and the letter you had wished would never come.

A RAGTIME TUNE

It was the dumbest debate I had ever heard.

A distraction.

A pause in the protest designed to ignite a shit storm from the hairy men sat whispering amongst themselves in a dreary fugue of cigar smoke, distressed mahogany, and glasses full of liquid fire. A ritual gone wrong, some might say. It was only a matter of time before someone cried foul. They'd all played the game at one time or another, had all ridden the rails through back country shanty towns, their harps swooning over a sadness none of them would ever admit to. They'd all suffered and survived long dark nights and even longer days of grey cement, razor wire, and a thousand prayers left unwritten.

"Whatd'ya make of that?" asked one man to the other, confident his philosophy of single notes and walking bass lines, all in good time, would have him survive the whole embarrassing affair. "It's about oppression," he claimed, thinking no one in this cotton-pickin' joint could deny that.

"I ain't denying nothin'," replied the other as he reached over and rooked his opponent out of a Queen. "It's about hard drivin' rhythm, you know, passion and heat and women thick in the thigh, battin' their chocolate browns at you."

"No it ain't," cried another from the back of the crowded room. "It's about pain. Fresh, startling, and insistent. Real juke joint piss water and poverty."

Everyone started cheering and stomping their feet until the bare bulbs were swinging and flickering overhead. That's when the last man stood up, slammed his whiskey down his throat, then adjusted his hat before walking up to the rickety old gaming table. He stood there a spell, his pinstripe suit melting into the shadows. Before speaking one word, he leaned in and put his smoldering cigar out in one of the men's glass of beer. "And you lot call yourselves musicians," he said with a bit of a toothless smile set upon a worn and weary face. "It's about the perfect fourth. It's about the sacrifice, isn't it? ... It's about the blow and the draw ... and clean underwear when you need it. And don't let that cracker-jack at the crossroads tell you otherwise."

No one had seen the tall man with the white patent leather shoes enter the joint, and no one saw him leave, but they all knew he was right, so they put their harps away and went back to arguing about chess.

CONFESSIONS

"What happens in Vegas stays in Vegas," replied Satan as he leaned in to place the angel atop the tree. Its wings were made of tin foil, and they crinkled in the hot breeze, so he reached out a little farther. The ladder teetered slightly, swayed slightly more, one hoofed foot thrown out to gaiety the other navigating the flaming abyss below via the uppermost step. You wanted to say something, anything at all, but the small hairy midgets kept handing you martini glasses full of tomato juice and black olives. You see, that hotel room had become a prison cell, and Elvis your Rabbi, reciting the last rights in a white leisure suit, all swinging hips and patent leather shoes. You had gone there alone, a tramp, hitchhiking the desert roads drawn like a firefly to the hypnotizing twinkle of oppression. Had gone to shake your moneymaker for any lunatic with a nickel, but your box wasn't a jewel box and the shiv in your hand was nothing more than a shattered piece of glass wrapped in a bit of tin.

"What did you expect, girl?" Satan asked of you again, his voice cocooned in nectar. "Did you think you'd like it better here? I read your diary, so I know. I know you. Nothing makes any sense to you anymore, not like it did when you were in France, when you kissed that woman twice your age. She barely had a pulse, and you, a loaded rifle and a cheering crowd. So hand me the tinsel ... and have another drink. 'Tis the season's eternal down here."

MADE IN CHINA

You had run away, slunk away into the blackness of the night, back to factory that made you. The paint had faded from your lips, and the threads of your linen frock had come undone, tangled and unruly, like the glorious dreams you once had, packaged in pink vellum and butterflies, licking salty flowers with their wings.

But now the wind howls, and the giant cockroach sings. That factory is gone, all rusted out steel and labor pains. Smoke rises from a small wood fire, nothing but chalk and charcoal left, greying the rouge ... of all that remains.

SNAKE OIL

The large photograph tacked to the wall said GOT LICE with the steel-eyed stare of a snake charmer, all sepia-toned, locked-jawed sneer and snarl. The line circling the gypsy wagon trailed off at least a mile into the shadows of the wood: the marks all shining lemonade smiles and shuffling feet, the deep-drawn creases at their eyes and mouths hiding shameful secrets and the misery of too little sleep.

"It won't take much. Just a wee drop for a sixpence," said the hunch-backed old crone to each in turn as she stuffed the last of their resolve into her pockets. Her hands reached deep, deep enough to touch the smooth teeth of all the little children gone lost on this dusty, dirty old street.

CRYSTALLINE ASPHYXIA

So there I was, sitting on a dirt floor in this musty old Mexican jail cell. I knew I shouldn't have shot my dog, knew it before I pulled the trigger. Knew it before I had even loaded the greasy black barrel.

Sitting on a burnt out sofa across from me are two tramps, their legs spread wide, licking at the last drops of water from a jug as if it were a drifting grape jamboree. They were like me. One day they had arrived, and one day they were gone, just like my dog. I shouldn't have shot him in the head, but he was a drunk bastard, all shimmering white teeth and no manners. He panicked the tourists, so what else could I do?

GLASS COFFIN

The metronome clicked and clacked in time to the beating of my heart. They took me while I was sweeping the stoop of my shop. I never saw the garden, never saw the heart-struck lovers writing their names with wild rapture upon the walls of the Governor's tomb. I've been selling those crayons for years – the red and brown ones mostly – but only to children, always tiptoeing in around the counter in their crisp linen and starbrite smiles. I asked for an opera, my last wish, you see, and they found one I fancied, but the gramophone is old ... shabby and old, like me. All the string instruments sound of whingeing in a tunnel, out of tune and strained with impatience, but at least it drowns out the idle humming of the executioner, and all the dull scraping of stone against steel.

MULE

You used to eat them, the scabs, and the fleas, picked them and flicked them and then liked to lick them — lick their smashed little heads off the tip of your index finger. But that was before they came, an unwanted knock at the door. You could see their sulky shadows, like smoke, drifting back and forth, jiggling the door handle. You can remember how cold the tile was and how it stunk of bleach and urine. The nurses — tight hair and tight faces — had come earlier with their cattle prods and calipers, all smiling and pushing babies in strollers. It was always the same thing — head back, eyes forward, let me see under your tongue — like you were some kind of derelict carnival ride held together with paranoia and graffiti. You'd been to the Garden of Eden. You told them that, a thousand times. It wasn't a lie. You had seen the fields of flowers, had drunk of their sacred milk. How you longed for that garden again ... and the tender innocence of green hills and the dawn.

THE VIRGIN, THE SERPENT, AND THE GREAT LIE

It was like holding a snake on a leash, this idea I had of beauty and truth. I'd wrestled with it often, and once, it won, dragged me off until I found myself lost in a dream. A waking dream. Where I had not a stitch of clothing with which to bind my thoughts.

It was dark, the trees black and barren, and the snow was blowing hard, a dusting of ice coating my every stifled breath. I had forgotten my name, or maybe it was that I never had one. For that moment in time, I was a stranger, stumbling towards a light at the end of a distant road.

The tavern windows were aglow, and the mood merry. There was talk tainted of Proustian contemplations lifted up upon airy voices into dark corners and empty spaces. There were mouths full of good bread and prayer and bowls full of warm broth and argument. No one was starving there, in that quiet village I had found by chance.

No one was naked or frail ... No one except me.

METABOLIC SYNDROME

The lake was warm – silent, still, and warm – warmer than it should have been, even for August in the desert. The desert looks the same as it did, before the event and the fatigue that followed. I like how they call it THE FATIGUE instead of saying what they really mean. But no one says what they really mean anymore. We don't have to ... the disease spread so fast. I can still smell it, the pungent taste of it on what's left of my tongue – the taste of rot and charred flesh. Then the body scanners came, talking of injections and radiation, threats and risk, all wrapped up in purple velvet quotations so we wouldn't notice when things got weird, when things began to change. Even an idle thought could condemn: at best a padded room, or at worst, a bullet in the throat or in the head. I'm not sure which was the better option. I'm not sure the word option has any meaning anymore. Living has become so ... so not like living. There's no pulse, no breath, no more tea and fresh figs. We're all feeding on the afterbirth, pawning stolen memories and marking the end of all things with bits of popcorn and string. It was the shame that did us in. "Yes," I thought in shouted words as I stuck myself with the needle for the seventeen millionth time. "It wasn't the hatred. It was definitely the shame."

TRODDEN UPON

He asked if I would "let him gnaw" on my pig bone. He didn't say it exactly in so many words, but I wasn't clueless: I knew what he meant. We'd got drunk together more than once on a thimble full of whiskey. We'd pissed and we'd shit together, and heck, we'd even sharpened our pitch forks and lit the petrol on the torches together. That's the way it was for us, all spit shines and have you got a quarter to spare. He was a deft one, he was, although I wasn't exactly sure what that meant. I believed it 'cause he told me so; showed me what it meant once — in a book — but I can't read. It's not a bad thing. I don't get confused by a lot of meanings, you see. That's how I knew he was hungry, 'cause I was too.

THINGS YOU CARRY

It was a cold wet sensation she felt behind her eyes, not like a suicide attack of tunnel vision but more of a rising pressure in her blood, pushing against her temples. She'd paced the corridor about a hundred or so times since dawn, a vial of radioactive water in one hand, her corroded dreams suspended in a vial of bacterium in the other. She'd gotten caught up in all the little irrelevant details and had left much unwritten, unsaid, and unthought. "What you say can be used against you." She laughed with her whole body, trembling, a sucker-punch bordering on the fringe of despair, and then she thought of the tumor growing inside her. Lymphoma, Carcinoma, Sarcoma ... all those things you carry that can't be cut loose with a pipe bomb or a machete. All those little insignificant things that dig in and bury themselves in your flesh. She'd met herself once, a long time ago — before the malignancy. It was late in the evening: an airport, a small smoking lounge with leather chairs, bad art, and a vodka martini with a new twist. She shook her own hand with a firm grip as if she knew the sickness had claimed another — had already ruined her. One of the vials cracked in her clenched fist, but she couldn't remember which one was which.

PIGEON

You twisted the plastic rod, closing the shabby Venetian blinds until the slivers of noonday sun could no longer lacerate your shadowed flesh or cast aspersions at the velvet wallpaper, the cheap art-deco ashtrays, or the dirty sheets.

You weren't where you wanted to be, but the clock was ticking.

You closed your eyes and stared at the red dots shape-shifting against the back of your eyelids. You still had the fetid taste of him in your mouth. His fingers were salty – greasy – and the area inside your cheek where they had swabbed felt like raw meat when your tongue accidentally brushed against it as you spoke. You hadn't been vaccinated. Had refused. It was a tricky diagnosis and an even trickier recipe. Cocktail, they liked to call it. The barcode on your arm said REFUGEE, but it was harvest time. They were trafficking in limbo, and we had all been preached the tenets. The lies were thrilling, the truth – a brazen assault. We were ill-equipped to fight, and the meds didn't work anymore god damn it.

Not for any of us.

ANYONE FOR SQUIRREL?

They serve slop in the galley. The sort of overly rendered fatty crap you had to paddle your way through before your stomach got wise and aborted the unmentionable shit as if you ate a toxic bag of medical sharps. Broccoli and cheese mash soup served over urinal cake. It had a curious citrus scent soaked in forest fire. "This tastes lovely," my wife said aloud so that Greta the Nazi chef could hear her over the squirming and squealing in the soup pot. "Did you have a nice day, dear?"

I hadn't, and I really didn't feel the need to reciprocate the nicety since she'd obviously spent the day with prince valium, and I couldn't care less.

I'd had to swallow my fifth rejection that day. My mouth already tasted like ass, so what did it matter. Greta was the housekeeper. She loved to cook, and my wife loved it because she couldn't. Every night we ate rare and exotic dishes from the old country: our backyard. "Put hair on your chest," Greta always said while pounding her sagging tits lower on her torso than even gravity could manage. My wife loved a hairy chest. I didn't have one. Over the years, it had migrated to my back. My wife didn't seem to notice, like she didn't notice the dead cat on the lawn or the hair in the soup. I suppose even if she did, she wouldn't care. She'd puke it up later anyway and then wash the taste out of her mouth with a bit of vodka. I wish she'd suck my johnson like she sucks on that twist of lime. I stabbed what was moving on my plate and then looked over at my son in his droopy socks and scuffed patent leather shoes, who sat there pinning roaches to a napkin with map tacks.

"Don't play with your food, sweetie." My wife has the maternal conviction of a hot dog with rigor mortis, so my son just smiled at his mother, put a live one in his mouth, and started crunching to the rhythm of whatever pop nonsense bullshit he was listening to. The boy wanted nothing to do with the conversation. He didn't understand what a nice day was. A nice day for him was picking scabs, and he once proclaimed after calling me an old fart, that I should know that better than anyone.

UNFILTERED RAGWEED

At some point or another in his life, he'd tried to smoke just about everything from urine soaked carpet fibers, to cat mint, to his favorite unwashed socks. Two packs a day, every day, three hundred and sixty-five days a year. The thought astounded him, since he never seemed to have a light. Consequently, it had been a long time since he'd had eyebrows; couldn't even remember what he'd looked like when he had. The phrase "Smoke em if you got em," was an invitation that could not be refused, even if he hadn't got em. Anything would do, and the trail of damage was evident; yet, he conceded to it as if it were little more than a pyromaniac's love of sport killing. Nothing was terrifying enough to overshadow the need he felt, not even the chorus of critics with their online hit man plots. He knew he'd suffer, like any true artiste, but he knew how to get away with it, knew how to throw it all off. Knew how to spark it fierce in secret, and how to inhale until he got the sense of another consciousness filtering the void. He knew it was growing — darkening all the soft tissues — that need taken physical form, but it was too late. From the first, he'd always known ... it was just too late.

300 DAYS OF POLYESTER STARSHINE

It was the little black dress. The way the static electricity clung to it, to me. I was a walking stun gun waitin' to discharge.

That was back in the day, though, when I'd found it – the dress – hanging out of a dumpster down at the end of a dark sticky alley I used to dive. Over off Easton Street, I think. It fit me like a glove, a black glove of toil and compassion, and it seemed to just disappear in the night when I held it up to my body, when I pressed it to my side, and for a brief moment in time, my miserable life felt just like a dream, all starry-eyed nights, champagne, velvet, and moonlight ... when the city smog lay close to the pavement, churning and swirling in the hot hair from the steam grates. The gaslights seemed like spotlights, and it was snowing chips of peppermint crystal. I can remember it in my hair as I posed this way and that, provocatively for the camera. The photographer said he was an everyman's tour guide, looking for a five-way swap. He said he was always looking for the better, the elusive, the impossible. Said I had it and that he wanted it. Said I was addictive and could be a star ... but it was just the dress.

I blamed it a lot for the way I felt about myself, about everything. I had called it a bargain once. Didn't really feel bad about it then, but in this over-the-counter-miracle-tonic culture, I can see how a word like that could hurt.

It said, "be gentle" and "dry flat" at some point in reply.

This was early in our relationship, our esteem for each other unmolested, but those words, those words like everything else on the street, would fray and fade over time.

CORPSE SAFARI

I just love the way this cemetery looks at dusk, all hard edges, soft porn, and the tacky neon glow of a theme park crushed up against a Cezanne sky. The Ubiquitous Mr. Lovegroove had come to collect on a debt. "Thirteen," he had whispered into the other end of the line. When I didn't answer, "Thirteen," he said again in his superfly-slick platform accent, and I could hear him take a long drag from his cigarillo. I imagined it smelled like cherry liqueur. That's how I'd got myself into this awful mess. I was addicted to infomercials, chocolate, and alternative analgesics. Dark dirty things. I wasn't alone though. Wasn't the only Queen protesting the hourly rate. What's a girl to do but wait on that million dollar briefcase? The kind that comes with a three-piece suit and shines like a narcotic crash kit. It happens. When you've been pushed to the edge and motivation's got a stiff grip on your throat, you'll lie, you'll cheat, you'll steal, and you'll blame yourself for it until your head's gone numb. We've all been on that street corner, the intersection between living and dying, peddling our asses for a bit of loose change. It's a crap shoot. Some hit the big time – free buffets and complimentary suites – but most wind up out in the desert, wandering the graves with nothing but the howling coyote moon to light their way.

ELEVATOR SHAFT

I was in a hurry to get up to my room. I hated business travel, but the swanky hotel bars made every trip just bearable. I shouted, "Wait," and a slender calf in red leather pumps jutted out to stop the elevator doors from closing. I stumbled in, tripping over my bag, my open umbrella, and my own damn feet. My new oxfords hurt my feet something awful, but they looked sharp, and for this meeting later today, I had to look sharp. I looked over at the leg and said, "Thanks." Then I shook the rain out of my hair and straightened out my tie.

"You're welcome," she said. "Name's Jim, as in slim ... 'cause I like a little spicy beef."

I wasn't sure I had heard her right. Maybe I had rain in my ears. They hadn't popped since I got off the damn plane.

"Yeah, you heard me right," she said while chewing on the second or third Cheeto she'd popped into her mouth. Her fingers were orange, and so was the lacy push-up bra that had pushed its way clear up to her chin. Orange like that creamsicle ice cream I used to love as a kid. She was young, very pretty in a sass-your-ass sort of way, perky tits, and I felt my face get a little hot. Even if I had had one word rattling around in my head at that moment, I wouldn't have been able to articulate it, so I spent about five minutes admiring the carpet and the advantages of having such a busy pattern in an area that obviously saw a lot of filth. The advantages of such a thing were so many that I completely forgot what floor my room was on. She picked a floor for me, and in doing so, shifted her ass in such a way that the very short apple-green suede skirt she was wearing slid all the way up to her shoulders. I got a premium view of her in the overhead mirror. It, too, was dusted Cheeto orange.

She bent over a little more and wiggled herself at me. I thought I was gonna pass out. Why are elevators so hot? Maybe I have malaria.

"Whatta ya waiting for?" she asked, but there was no conceivably logical answer I could find that wasn't scribbled on the inside of my boxers. I reached out with one finger and touched her. Then, she told me to go ahead and taste it, so I put my finger in my mouth, and I'll be damned if it didn't taste like a Cheeto. She smiled at me, so I grabbed her hips and went for it like they teach you in all those stupid business assertiveness classes. She gasped and her head hit the wall.

For about five minutes, the elevator pitched and bowed, swinging so wildly on its cables that I thought for sure we were gonna die. Yeah! Fuck that meeting. Fuck shitty air travel. Fuck my boss, and fuck his boss with the rolled up presentation I had in my briefcase. I just wanted to die right then and there.

She didn't say a word.

The doors opened just as I was zipping up in a fluster. I could taste Cheeto on my tongue. I got off, no idea what fucking floor, as another suit got in, and just as the doors were closing, I could hear the crinkle of another Cheeto packet and the low whisper of her sexy sultry voice, "Name's Jim, as in slim ... 'cause I like a little spicy beef."

VICTORIA'S EVEN BIGGER SECRET

Sometimes my cleavage gets in the way. I know I know. Sing me a sob story, but it's true. I can't always tell if my fly is undone, or if there's toilet paper stuck to my shoe, and it takes a wish and a prayer to find a suitable seat on the train where you're not rubbing against someone in an inappropriate manner. My boyfriend said, "The aftershocks rattled his brain" when we made love, and then I'd pass out cold, and he'd light an incense stick and let it burn between them 'cause he said the room smelled like flap sweat. I have hot ash scars on my chest to prove it. One of these days, I'm going to stick firecrackers in his ass-cheeks and light him up while he's sleeping in the cheap motel room he always takes me to. No one will notice with all the gunshots ricocheting off the cars in the parking lot. He's not really mean, my boyfriend, once you get to know him. He has a hearsay history of violence: spring rage chaos and polka dot blotter extremes. He's a backdoor gangsta now, all cat claws and camp, dealing a marked deck to the strip-club counselors, waiting out their fortunes in the mirrored velvet. He said he was built to bounce heads on concrete. I believed him, even if no one else did.

Once a month, he'd go through the motions: "Convict," his parole officer would call him, to which "hard knocks," he'd reply, and then, later, he'd curse my double Ds for knocking over his beer. If I had a ladder, I might climb it and hang myself by the nipples from the electrical wires adjacent to my fourth floor patio, hoping they and all the flabby skin attached to them would just rip right off. He said my tits were to blame for the fights and the bruises. Said I was just a tramp with a park side view and a short commute when all he had was a brick wall and an alley. All I know about views is that the paint's chipping on the ceiling, and the palm trees behind the couch are fake, like those boxed potatoes he loves so much that would crust up in his beard for a week. It made his face rough, but he'd just yell over my chest and tell me to "shut up, hang on, and ride it out."

In the evenings, after he was through with me, I'd take a bath, but could never reach my legs to shave them, so I'd lie there, watching my breasts flap and swish around in the steamy water and wonder how much it would hurt if I just sliced them off.

STEM CELLS AND SNAKE SKIN POLE DANCERS

Big brother was my knight in shining armor. Tin foil and duct tape — he was a lunatic wanted to influence the common things for the common people. Take a pill, shut your eyes, read a third grade primer. He'd kick the bricks whenever I complained that I wanted to play outside. "Our houses are made of mud, see?" he'd say, "And sex is a landmine like raw meat and weed killer." Then he would declare out of nowhere: This is my last inquest. Alert the riot police! But it was never his last. He told me once, in a whisper, that innuendo takes refuge in the smoking lounges next to the lizards in three-piece Dolce suits. I laughed, and he slapped me. I didn't think lizards had enough fingers and thumbs to button all those buttons, but he was convinced, so we'd spent a lifetime hiding our sins.

It's not a lie if you believe it yourself.

The lies, what I liked to call our melancholy moments together, lasted years. Days and hours more than I wanted them to. Our words like phantoms in the fog, we'd scroll through bus schedules looking for the last stop. He'd make a difference one day. He said our souls were windowless; our promises: nothing but rosy breath, swollen with honeydew from a thousand trampled weeds. "You have no imagination," he'd say to me as we watched the static on the color TV, and I would ask, "What's that?" because whatever it was, he had never allowed me to have one.

CLOCKS

You used to have to wait, wanting like a hunter, alive with wilderness and morning dew in your veins. You hated it – the waiting – but now, the card cast at your feet betrays the anticipation you once felt. The hanged man reflects back into you, a smile of idle contentment upon his face. The iridescent rainbow of your childish dreams is nowhere to be seen.

A church burns in a damp meadow.

And you have no tobacco left to smoke after the great feast.

"What is the answer?" you ask the shadows now collecting at your feet, but they too are tired of waiting – for you. There is nothing at the end of it all, their boney fingers pointing away into the darkness just beyond your breath. Nothing, they whisper as their writhing vestments pull and tug at your flesh. Nothing but an alley in the cold loneliness of the night, where time aims to mock you, drip, drip, dripping from the cement walls as this imaginary prison becomes your life.

CAULDRON

It was such a clear night, the moonlight dancing through the crests of the trees, the wind nothing more than a crinkling shiver through the dry leaves.

A sailor returned to the shoreline of his death, bare feet sunk in the sand, collecting the rotten bits of fish and seaweed that pushed and pulled at his ankles with the urgency of the tide.

He couldn't stop them.

Not in his own lifetime.

Not that he hadn't tried to douse the fire with selfish lament and prayer, but even then, he couldn't stop them clinging to their hatred and despair.

"Too young," he said to the small fish lying lifeless in his wet hand. "You're too young, and I'm too old and alone to strip any meat from the well-worn bone."

ABOUT THE AUTHOR

Cheryl Anne Gardner is a writer of dark, often disturbing art-house novellas and abstract flash fiction. Her love of literature began at an early age with Stoker's Dracula. Captivated by the Gothic and Dark Romantic stylings of Poe, Lovecraft, Kafka, and de Sade, her passion for the macabre manifests itself throughout her own work to this day. In 2010, she became enamored with Flash Fiction and its experimental style, and she's been writing prolifically in the genre ever since. She enjoys exploring political, social, and psychological issues. Her flash fiction has been published in dozens of journals. When she isn't writing, she likes to chase marbles on a glass floor, eat lint, play with sharp objects, and make taxidermy dioramas with dead flies. She lives with her husband and ferrets on the east coast USA, is an enthusiastic gardener, and dabbles in cement sculpture when she isn't spoiling her adopted feral cat.

You can find her work at Twisted Knickers Publications and various online retailers. Her novellas are available in print and in eBook formats. Titles include:

And Death Dreamt Us All
The Thin Wall
Logos
The Splendor of Antiquity
The Kissing Room

THE CREDITS

300 Days of Polyester Starshine . (2012, February). *Conotation Press An Online Artifact*
A Distant Afternoon. (2011, July 1). *Negative Suck*
A Murder on the Banks of the Seine . (2011, October 3). *The Carnage Conservatory*
A Ragtime Tune . (2011, Issue 7). *Thunderclap Magazine*
A Sack of Rags and Rocks. (2011, September 1, Issue Deliria). *Danse Macabre*
A Walk Down Avenue des Champs-elysees . (2011, October 31). *In Between Altered States*
Acapulco in Winter . (2012, February). *Pure Slush - Counterpoint*
Aliceblue. (2011, June 3, Summer Nights Issue). *Danse Macabre*
Anyone for Squirrel? . (2012, February 17). *Weirdyear*
Beware of Dog. (2011, May 12). *The Carnage Conservatory*
Bike Trails and Ash Clouds. (2011, November/December Issue II). *Stone Highway Review*
Bleeder. (2011, November 3). *The Carnage Conservatory*
Broken. (2012, Volume 1.3) *Downer Magazine*
Choke. (2012, January Winter Edition). *Menacing Hedge*
Chrome Bumpers . (2012, January). *Thirteen Myna Birds*
Cinema Noir. (2011, August). *Let's Fuck Later [Out of Print]*
Confessions. (2011, October). *Three Minute Plastic*
Corpse Safari . (2012, February 10). *Furious Fictions*
Debt Collectors. (2012, July 13). *The Carnage Conservatory*
Deputy Larry. (2011, September 5). *Amphibi.us*
Doll Heads. (2011, June 6). *The Carnage Conservatory*
Elevator Shaft. (2012, February 1). *Hobo Pancakes*

Eligible Bachelor . (2011, October 10). *The Carnage Conservatory*
Flashcard Freestyle and that wicked, wicked Bandwidth. (2012, January 21). *Linguistic Erosion*
Fractured Radiant. (2011, June 7). *The Carnage Conservatory*
Ghosts in Winter. (2011, September 16). *The Carnage Conservatory*
Glass Coffin . (2011, December Featured Author). *Negative Suck*
Hey Shitbag! What's My Destiny. (2011, July 26). *The Carnage Conservatory*
Hyperthyroidism. (2011, July 28). *In Between Altered States*
In Flight Entertainment. (2011, May 15). *Pure Slush*
Intern. (2011, September). *Let's Fuck Later [Out of Print]*
Lessons from The Gridiron: Voyeurism and Gingivitis . (2011, September). *Pure Slush Print Edition: Slut*
Lithium and Gin. (2011, June 8). *Dark Chaos [Out of Print]*
Madame Malicious and The Most Unlikely of Peers . (2012, February 7). *The Carnage Conservatory*
Made in China . (2011, December Featured Author). *Negative Suck*
Margaritas and Razor Blades: After Five Porno for Skeptics . (2011, June 22). *The Carnage Conservatory*
Me, You, and They. (2011, August 6). *The Carnage Conservatory*
Metabolic Syndrome . (2011, December Featured Author). *Negative Suck*
Moratorium. (2011, August 11). *Let's Fuck Later [Out of Print]*
Mule. (2011, December Featured Author). *Negative Suck*
Muse. (2011, July). *Let's Fuck Later [Out of Print]*
Name's Ted. Can I Help You With Your Baggage? .

(2012). *The Carnage Conservatory*
Parked Cars. (2012, Issue 31). *Yellow Mama*
Persian Cat. (2011, April 10). *d.ustb.in*
Pigeon. (2011, December Featured Author). *Negative Suck*
Provincial Love and Ether . (2011, November 28). *In Between Altered States*
Rancid Dusk. (2012, Februrary 23). *Flash Fiction Offensive*
Raw Sewage . (2012, January). *Thirteen Myna Birds*
Red Lights and Jade Paint . (2011, December 23). *The Carnage Conservatory*
Red Riding. (2011, October 14). *The Carnage Conservatory*
Relapse. (2011, May 26). *The Carnage Conservatory*
Schedule C. (2011, May 15). *The Molotov Cocktail*
Scoop of Clotted Cream with Bugs. (2011, June 15). *The Carnage Conservatory*
Snake Oil . (2011, December Featured Author). *Negative Suck*
Spanish Limes. (2011, June 1). *Pure Slush*
The Clipper, The Clown, and A Bag of Dark Dirty Things. (2011, September 24). *The Carnage Conservatory*
The Disquiet of Dorian and The Grey . (2012, January 24). *The Carnage Conservatory*
The DuskHouse. (2011, June 24). *In Between Altered States*
The Kitchen Sink. (2011, July 1). *Postcard Shorts*
The Legacy and a Hot Pink Eddy. (2011, September 27). *The Carnage Conservatory*
The Shadow Factory. (2011, July 1). *The Carnage Conservatory*
The Strange Sickness of Stan Worchkowsky . (2011, October Issue 14). *The Molotov Cocktail*
The Virgin, The Serpent, and The Great Lie . (2011,

December Featured Author). *Negative Suck*
Things You Carry . (2011, December Featured Author). *Negative Suck*
Trodden Upon . (2011, December Featured Author). *Negative Suck*
Unexpected Guests. (2012, September) *One Title*
Unfiltered Ragweed . (2012, February). *Conotation Press An Online Artifact*
Victoria's Even Bigger Secret. (2012, March 14). *Near to The Knuckle*
Water Cooler Nu Allonge. (2012, February). *Conotation Press An Online Artifact*
WD-Forty . (2011, December 13). *Daily Love*
What Sweet Music They Make. (2012, February 22). *The Carnage Conservatory*

AND DEATH DREAMT US ALL
A Novella

Her prose is full of lyricism and imagery that you will find both stunning and disturbing. — Amazon

The imagery is sublime, the tension palpable. If you love dark fiction you gotta get this book. — Bolt Cutter Design

Rowan is one deliciously haunted individual and the prose proves both dark and inviting. — Amazon

LOGOS
A Novella

Gardner's words kindle fires in the reader similar to dark woeful wordsmiths like Anne Rice and Poppy Z. Brite. Packs a powerful wallop. — Horror.com

Immersion into Gardner's macabre settings is inevitable for the reader. — BreeniBooks.com

A dark and richly detailed work. — Amazon

THE THIN WALL
A Novella

Both literary and erotic without being tacky or over-indulgent. — PODBRAM

Dark almost obsessive eroticism in the most romantic of tones. Convincing and unashamed. — Goodreads

A story that is both entertaining and frightening at the same time. — DactylReview

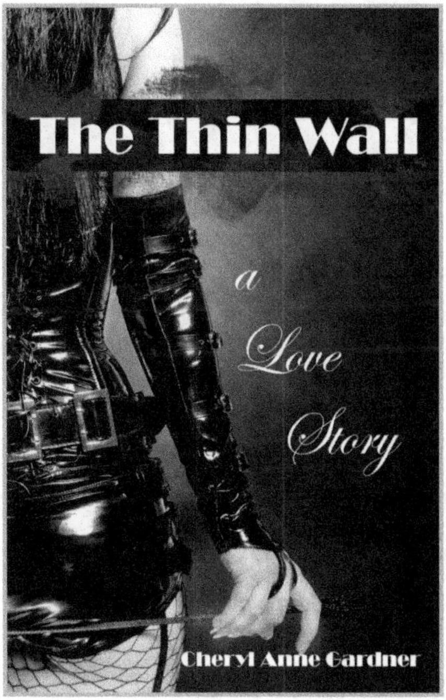

www.ingramcontent.com/pod-product-compliance
Lightning Source LLC
Chambersburg PA
CBHW071307130626
46556CB00004B/1512
9780991002719